THE WRANGLER

THE WRANGLER

THE YACHT CLUB SERIES
BOOK 2

JORDYN KROSS

This book contains descriptions of BDSM practices, but this is a work of fiction and should not be used as a guide to actual sexual practices. The author and publisher will not be responsible for any loss, harm, injury, or death resulting from the use of the information in this fictional work.

Published by Scarlet Parlor Press, LLC

Library of Congress Control Number: 2024921719

Publisher's Cataloging-in-Publication

(Provided by Cassidy Cataloguing Services, Inc.)

Names: Kross, Jordyn, author.
Title: The wrangler / Jordyn Kross.
Description: [Albuquerque, New Mexico] : Scarlet Parlor Press, LLC, [2024] | Series: The yacht club series ; book 2
Identifiers: ISBN: 978-1-959691-14-3 (paperback) | 978-1-959691-13-6 (ebook)
Subjects: LCSH: Man-woman relationships--Fiction. | Families--Fiction. | Forgiveness--Fiction. | Deception--Fiction. | Sadomasochism--Fiction. | LCGFT: Erotic fiction. | Romance fiction. | BISAC: FICTION / Romance / Erotic. | FICTION / Romance / Contemporary.
Classification: LCC: PS3611.R776 W73 2024 | DDC: 813/.6--dc23

Editors: Dayna Hart

Jenny Rardon

Cover: Brandi Doane McCann

Uhraervi Brothers

Open Enrollment

Hung with Care

Pole Position

NOAH Series

Prequel Novella - Quantum Entanglements

Book 1 - Captain's Treasure

Nonfiction

Demystifying the Beats

Single Titles

A Lost Claus

To my own Southern gentleman, who believes in second chances and has had me tied in knots from the beginning. XO always.

ONE

SJ

I park my rented red sports car in front of the brightly painted Sunflower Inn and blow out a steadying breath. I'm here for a reason. I can do this.

I push the car door open wide, pivot on the seat, and attempt a graceful exit in case anyone is watching. I walk back to the trunk on stiff legs, breathing in the warm summer air that carries an earthy pine scent. The long, mountainous drive from Denver International challenged me more than I expected. I pop open the back with a press of a button and gloat one last time about how I managed to fit both suitcases in the tiny space.

Leaving my extra-large bag for the moment, I retrieve my carry-on and wheel the case to the doorway of the repurposed Victorian. The website didn't capture how cute and welcoming the place would be.

A bell chimes when I open the unlocked cobalt blue front door. After I shift my bag across the threshold, I have to catch my breath. The room is stunning. Floor-to-ceiling windows on the far wall overlook an inviting patio before a grassy lawn leads to a towering embrace of evergreens. I've never seen anything like it.

"Welcome to the Sunflower. You must be Sonja." A friendly woman with a welcoming smile steps off the last stair to my left. "I'm Amy. I'm so happy you found us."

I smile back. "Your directions were perfect."

"I'm glad." She moves behind a tall wooden cabinet topped with a crocheted doily on top, an open guest book, and a small vase of flowers. "I have a room ready for you. It overlooks the back garden, so you should have plenty of quiet for your writing. It's so exciting to have a writer staying here." She leans forward conspiratorially. "I'm an avid reader, so you'll have to share your pen name with me before you leave."

A nervous laugh escapes my lips. "Of course."

"Your agent called earlier, and the payment is taken care of. He prepaid four weeks but said you might need to stay over. It's not a problem at all. I blocked out the room for two months." Amy fusses in the drawers of the cabinet.

The front door opens, and I glance over my shoulder to catch a heartbreak of a man walking in. Sunlight from the huge windows illuminates the golden streaks in his tousled hair. His tight white tee, baring evidence of his day's work, stretches over a plane of abs that look like an impossible drawing. His faded jeans are filled with the promise of breathtaking nights. I gasp in a breath and avert my eyes. He looks like a mortal sin I want to commit over and over again.

"Hey, Alex," Amy calls out.

His footsteps on the wood floor pause. "Amy. Ma'am."

I can't resist a second glimpse, confirming I'm truly in hell.

He nods in my direction. "How're y'all doing?"

His slow Texas twang twists its way between my legs. I'm dying. I'm supposed to focus on writing my debut novel. My uncle sent me to get away from all the distractions. He's given me a gift I can't repay, and already I'm distracted by this dream man.

Who looks vaguely familiar.

"This is Sonja Redding. She's staying with us for a few weeks."

He grunts his acknowledgement, and I flinch at the name my uncle selected. He said I had to use a cover. Sounded cool and mysterious at the time. Seems ridiculous now.

I turn to face the temptation who could derail my entire reason for being in Colorado. "Hi, Alex."

His gaze travels up and down my body, but he's got a deer-in-the-headlights vibe. All shock and avoidance. Never had that reaction.

"Since you're going up, could you show her to the Columbine room?" Amy hands me a key with a blue flower tag.

"Yes, ma'am." He points at me. "That your bag?"

Yes, that is my vag. I blink. *Bag.* He said bag. "I can get it."

"No, ma'am." He snatches the case and takes it hostage, heading for the stairs.

I'm halfway up the flight, mesmerized by the muscles in his legs and ass. I have to say something. "You work construction?"

"Yes, ma'am. And you?" he asks without looking back. He tops the stairs and heads down the wide welcoming hallway dotted with closed doors on either side.

I give him the story I'm supposed to, although why my uncle doesn't want to take credit for such a generous gift is a mystery. "I'm a writer. My agent booked this place for me so I can finish a novel. I should have had it done months ago. He says it's to remove distractions."

He glances back. I dart my gaze away from his ass. So busted. He stops in front of the door marked Columbine and steps aside. I use the key Amy gave me to open it wide. I haven't been here a minute, and already I'm avoiding my purpose to pursue a man. What is wrong with me?

The room is lovely and inviting. Walls a pale lavender, more blue than pink. A huge bed done in white linens with big fluffy pillows and an accent throw that matches the walls. It's the kind of bed to spend all day in, naked with someone sexy.

"Anything else?"

His voice jolts me from my mini-fantasy, and my cheeks heat. "I, uh, have a bigger bag in the car..." And things I'd like to do to him, despite the fact I'm supposed to be focusing on my future.

"Sure." He holds out his hand. "Keys?"

I search my pocket, retrieving the rental key for him. His eyes are locked on my actions. On me. Like he'd like to get tangled in the sheets of my fantasy with me. I drop the keys in his open palm, making sure not to touch. I've barely spoken to him, and already I'm mentally climbing him like a tree.

"Be right back." He spins and darts out the door.

I follow him, pausing in my open doorway. He's headed away from the stairs to the last door on the opposite side of the hall. He opens the door with a key similar to the one Amy gave me. After a brief disappearance, he's back in the hallway without his tools. He freezes when he sees me staring. A brief moment, and then he rushes past me to the stairs. I'm like a hungry cat eyeing a bird in a cage when it comes to his ass.

Once he's out of sight, my brain reengages, and I retreat into my room.

The bathroom is beautiful. A claw foot tub calls to me. The paint above the white tile running halfway up the wall is a shade or two darker than the bedroom. A stack of fluffy white towels on a painted wicker chair adds to the air of country luxury. My kind of fancy.

I could get naked right now, run a bath, and leave my door ajar. Too obvious. Too desperate. Too wrong.

I return to the bedroom at the exact moment Alex knocks. Without missing a beat, I open the door and smile, and an image of us in the tub fills me with steamy heat, despite my repeated warnings to myself.

"Here you go." He has my huge suitcase next to him, and he's not even breathing hard from bringing it up the stairs.

I step back, inviting him in.

He pushes the bag over the threshold. "Have a nice stay."

Before I can say anything else, he spins on a boot heel and races back to his room. At least one of us still has blood making it to their brain. The snick of his lock echoes down the hall. Damn. I've been here five minutes, and already I'm scaring people.

Sex is not on the agenda. Writing my book. Changing my life.

But first, a long soak.

My phone rings before I can take a step.

I pick it up from the bedside table. *Uncle MD.*

"Hi, Uncle."

"Sarah Jane, are you at the inn?"

"Yes. It's beautiful, and my trip was great. But the four-hour drive through the mountains was rough." Why did he pick a place so far away? Only now do I wonder, and it's too rude to ask, like looking a gift horse in the mouth. But then, the receiver gets the dental bills. Yeah, I need a bath and to relax. My brain is getting squirrely.

"I saw the charge on my card and assumed you must be there."

Without him, I wouldn't have this opportunity, and despite being wrung out from the trip, I should express my gratitude. "Thank you, Uncle MD. This is beyond kind of you. I can't believe I get to write my book. I don't know how I'll ever repay you."

"While you're there, let me know if you meet a fellow named Alex Craig."

What? "Why's that?"

"I don't know if you remember, but your cousin dated him in high school, and he disappeared after I arrested him. Been looking for him for years."

Why is he bringing this up now? And yes, I met an Alex, but I don't know if he's Alex *Craig*. Even with the accent. And Alex seems like a nice man. I cough to chase away my nerves. "You think he's *here*?" Where you sent me by myself?

"He shouldn't be working anywhere. He should be in jail for ruining your cousin. Ruined her life. Ruined our family. He had her tied up, for God's sake."

"How did I not know about this? Was Alyss okay?" My cousin hadn't said a word. But we'd also started to drift apart when she stopped visiting for the summers a couple years earlier.

"We never recovered as a family. But you can help me out, right Sarah Jane?"

"I don't know how I would—"

"It's no big deal. Just let me know if you meet anyone with that name. I'll take it from there. I think you might owe me one small favor. Don't you?" His voice is kind, and the reminder of what he's done for me is enough to have me agreeing.

"Yes, sir." I drop onto the bed, unable to hold myself

upright any longer. It must be the long day of travel. I came here to write my book, but I can give my uncle a hand. "I'm on it. I can do this."

My uncle gives me some encouragement about writing my book before he hangs up.

A light knock at the door forces me to rise from the cocoon of the bed.

Amy stands in the hallway. "I forgot to tell you. The guys decided to grill tonight, and there'll be plenty if you'd like to join us." The woman's warm smile is so inviting but wasted on me.

"That's so kind of you, but I think I'm going to test out that beautiful tub and get some rest. Traveling took it out of me." And I don't have an ounce of energy left to smile for strangers.

"Of course, I completely understand. I'll see you in the morning for breakfast." She turns away, and I close the door.

Steamy hot water fills the tub around me. I bend my knees, sinking into the warmth. Despite my uncle's little request—it's really no big deal to find out someone's name —I have a dream month to write my book. And I have the perfect inspiration in the tall hunk of cowboy who's living down the hall. As long as I keep my hands on the keyboard and away from his body, I'll have all the time I need to start my writing career.

TWO

ALEX

My phone chimes with a text.

Stone: *Grills hot. Get your ass down here.*

Fuck. I can't avoid the new guest forever, but no way am I going downstairs commando in gray sweats. Even after my tension-relieving session in the shower. One look at that sweet redhead's peach of an ass packed into blue jeans, and everyone will be aware of my situation. Hell, my damn cock is twitching just from threat of seeing her. I'm so screwed.

I shove my pants down, frowning at the fucker who gets me in all kinds of trouble. After tugging on some boxer briefs, because every layer will help, I put on a clean pair of jeans. The hallway is clear when I step out. I pause at the Columbine door. Should I invite her to join us? There'll be plenty.

"Yes, sir." Her voice sounds submissive, slightly scared even. Does she have a boyfriend? "I'm on it. I can do this." Huh? Maybe she's talking to her agent about the book. If so, he must be pushing her pretty hard.

I resist the urge to knock. She'll be too vulnerable, and I'm already a mess over her. I leave her door and continue down the hall.

Amy is coming up the stairs. "Did you invite Sonja?"

"Oh, uh?" I glance back up the stairs.

"Men." She shakes her head. "I'll ask her."

I nod and keep moving. I can already hear the guys out back. The back door must be open. I rush down the stairs, ready for a beer and whatever Stone's cooking tonight.

I hit the deck and take a deep breath. Spring in Colorado is a whole lot cooler than what I grew up with. Supposedly it will get warm this summer. I'm not sure these folks understand what heat is.

"There he is." Tyler hands me an open bottle of some microbrew.

I know better than to ask. Questions lead to lectures on hops and barley and yeast and shit that don't matter. Either the beer tastes good, or it doesn't. This one isn't bad. I give him a smile and nod to let him know I approve of his choice.

I glance around. Eliot is sitting at the table alone nursing his beer. I take the chair across from him.

"How's the construction coming?" he asks.

"Wait," Stone interrupts, dropping a plate of grilled brats on the table next to a bag of kaiser rolls.

Amy pops out the back door, her arms stacked with side-dish containers and condiments. I jump up to help her, but Tyler beats me to it. With a cheesy little bow, I wing out my arm. "May I escort you to your seat, ma'am?"

Amy snort laughs and takes my arm. Tyler rolls his eyes. Dishes are passed around the table as we load our plates.

"Where's Sonja?" I ask quietly.

"She wasn't feeling up to it. Long travel day." Amy settles into the chair I pull out, and I breathe a sigh of relief. At least dinner will be stress-free.

"How's the construction coming, Alex?" Tyler spoons sauerkraut into his bun.

"Dude, you were just out there." I give him shit because I know he's got an ulterior motive for asking. The former G-man always has a hidden agenda. "We're wrapping up the first two condos. The three-bedroom by two-bedroom disability accessible units should be ready for inspection in two weeks. The first standard three-bedroom might be done at the same time. Or close enough for us to schedule a visit from the inspector."

Eliot turns his eagle-eyed gaze to me. "Three by two's ours?"

"Yep." I nod, unable to say more without choking up. I cover my emotion by taking a big bite of fancy hot dog.

"Good," Stone says, breaking the tension of remorse. "Guess we should start thinking about the soft opening for the club. Friends and family."

"Not sure you want to refer to anything around a BDSM club as soft."

I can't believe Amy let that drop.

Eliot chokes on his beer.

I cover my plate. "That's alcohol abuse."

Stone ignores our cutups. "Before we invite anyone, we've got to finalize the rules. We've been dancing around this issue for weeks. We're settling it tonight."

This explains why Stone called a "family" dinner on a Monday night. Suddenly, I'm no longer hungry.

"Background checks. Even for guests," Eliot starts as expected.

I passed the cursory investigation in St. Louis, but there's no guarantee I'll pass another. My mom says the sheriff still hates me and threatens her almost every week after church, demanding she tell him where I am. It's been almost exactly ten years; statute of limitations is about up. I'm pretty sure I'll be okay after that. But it's a risk. Politicians change laws all the time to get what they want. No one back home has more power than the sheriff. I'd rather not appear on his radar due to a sex club search. I take a sip of my beer and shove my paranoia back.

"We need to check the registered sex offender databases as part of that investigation." Tyler's tone invites no argument. "Not sure we could secure liability insurance without that precaution."

"No felons. No sex offenders. I'd even look at arrest records. I don't want some sketchy, skirt-the-law motherfucker being used to take down what we're building here." Eliot crosses his arms.

"I agree. We need to use our heads. Look at each applicant as an individual." I'm surprised Stone isn't arguing for iron clad, no-exceptions rules. "I've seen evil fuckers with squeaky clean records, and I've met salt-of-the-earth guys who got caught up in bad situations. I'm fine with outsourcing the basic search, especially for temporary guest passes. But for full-fledged club members who can have access to the private rooms? We need to do better than a simple records search." Stone takes a pull off his beer and, as he lowers the bottle, locks his steely gaze on me.

I freeze so I won't squirm.

"What do you think, Alex?" Stone asks.

The guys all turn to me. Even Amy is curious about my answer.

"Anyone can be arrested." I pause trying to give myself some emotional distance. "Doesn't make what they're accused of true." I lift one shoulder in a half-hearted shrug as if I'm not talking about my own situation.

"Let's put together the guest list for friends and family." Amy, ever the diplomat, refocuses the conversation. "Keep the list to those people we know well. If we need to expand the list to people we know less well, we can let them know we're running a basic background check before they'll be invited to attend. And in the meantime, you can get a lawyer to help you draw up the membership contracts and put the background check requirements in there."

"Agreed. Friends and family, soft opening, exclusive to who we know well." Stone might as well have slapped down the gavel.

"We have to invite Reed." Eliot says it like a challenge. The man has been edgy for months.

Stone nods in approval.

"And Blake."

I jump in and try to ease Eliot's other, unspoken concerns about his partner who nearly died and may not walk again. "Elevator will be ready. The inspector is coming this week."

Amy stands up. "I made pie."

Tyler pops up, grabs a couple empty plates. "I'll help you."

That man can't be ten feet from her. He may whip her ass on the regular, but she's got him by the balls. I push aside my envy and finish my beer.

"Now that we're getting close—scheduling the soft opening—we should think about how we'll put up the website." Eliot leans back in his chair and stares up at the still brilliant blue sky. "Thanks to Blake, we have the domain, but he's not interested in designing a website. Not his thing. We'll need a public section and password-protected, members-only part."

"Katherine could probably do it." The words hit my lips before my brain has a chance to tell me to shut up.

"Gabe's wife?" Eliot asks.

"What *about* Katherine?" Amy is at the door with a key lime pie decorated with whipped cream. My mouth waters.

"Thinking about hiring her to design our website." Stone takes the pie and places it on the table. Tyler sets the plates down next to it.

"Oh. That's a great idea. She hasn't had a lot of design work lately." Amy cuts the slices and doles them out. "Not that she needs a job, but she loves that kind of thing."

Good. Amy can take point on asking Katherine. Gabe hates it when she has web-design work. Less time with his wife. They're disgustingly in love. Or maybe it's just me who's disgusted because I'll never have that. I glance up at the house. Did the curtain on Sonja's window twitch? Is she listening to us?

Fire ants of unease scurry up my back. Why wouldn't she join us if she's so curious?

I head upstairs after explaining I need to get to the site early, since the architect will be there and she's a total ball-busting pain in my ass. As I open the door to my room, my phone rings with a video call from my mom. I can't help but smile as I answer. "Hi, Momma."

Her voice comes in digital chunks and her face is frozen, only partially displayed on my screen. Shoot.

"Let me call you back." I hang up and voice call her, cursing the fact that high-speed internet still isn't available at the ranch. She answers right away and puts me on speaker. "Daddy's here too. Sorry about the video. I had to try."

"No problem. Hey, Daddy."

"Son, how're you doing?" It's been a couple weeks since we've spoken.

"Good. Staying busy with the construction. How about you?"

"We had to call you. It's so exciting," Momma bursts

out, sounding like a little kid. "Your daddy is officially on the ballot to run for sheriff."

"You are? When did you decide that?"

"Got tired of the sheriff bullying your momma. Neighbors got together and secured the signatures I needed to be on the ballot. So I guess I'm running."

I'm speechless. I have no idea what it will mean if Daddy wins. But I'm happy and proud of him for running. I tell him so and catch up on the news of the ranch. Before long, I'm yawning into the phone.

"We'll let you go, son," Momma says, recognizing I'm probably half asleep already.

"Love you," I mumble, and they reply before I end the call. I miss them more than phone calls can fix, but it's better than nothing.

THREE

ALEX

I'm late. The big dinner and stress of talking about the rules for the club gave me a sleepless night. I rub my eyes as I head down the stairs, my hair still damp from the quick shower I took to wake up. Gonna have to be careful with the power tools today.

Breakfast is laid out on the buffet. The number of hotplates and warmers is impressive. Amy still cooks for us like we're guests. Stone and Tyler are filling their faces. Amy comes out of the kitchen with a carafe in one hand.

"You're here." She stops next to me. "I assumed you'd already left for the site."

"Should've."

"Coffee?"

I nod, and she fills a mug for me. "I'll put it on the table."

I set my jaw when she places the cup at the empty

place next to Sonja. Not a problem. I'll just keep my head down, eat, and leave. With a clack of the tongs, I find space for two more slices of bacon on my loaded plate. Once the lid is back in place, covering the dish of the few remaining pieces, I turn to face the gorgeous redhead I should be avoiding. I don't want to make small talk. I don't want to ask her where she's from. I don't want to keep arguing with my dick about what a good idea it would be to get inside her. The DFW airline tags on her bags were all the warning I need.

Besides, brightly colored animals are dangerous.

Amy's chatting away so I don't say a word when I place my plate and take my seat. I shovel in the delicious food with less appreciation than it deserves. I can't spend too long around the woman next to me. She smells better than the bacon and coffee. My mouth is watering for all the wrong reasons.

"What kind of books do you write?" Amy asks, and I can't help but wait for the answer. Why do I care? It's not like I'm gonna buy her book and beg her to sign it. I shovel in another mouthful.

"Romance." Her cheeks turn a cute shade of pink. She probably writes those sweet historicals my momma likes.

"I used to read a lot of romance back in the day." Stone could have said he likes to paint his toenails pink and I wouldn't have been more surprised. "We used to pass them around my unit while waiting for things to happen. What kind of romance do you write?"

She puffs up her chest, lifting her breasts unnecessarily. "Contemporary erotic romance. BDSM."

I choke as my eggs go down the wrong pipe. A gulp of coffee clears up the mess enough for me to speak. "What do *you* know about BDSM?"

Everyone at the table is staring at me. I probably could have worded that question better or used a softer tone. But seriously, what the fuck does this woman know about bondage and submission? And why am I so desperate to hear her answer?

The pink of her cheeks darkens to a shade only a true redhead can achieve. An image of her naked with a red thatch between her legs flashes through my mind. What the fuck is this woman doing to me?

"I do a ton of research online. I get on the forums and talk to people who are in the lifestyle." She drags her fork through what's left of the eggs on her plate. "Without the funds to travel and no one to take me to a club—I do the best I can. It's difficult. My book has me all tangled up."

The naked Sonja in my brain is now encased in my ropes with beautiful knots, perfectly placed. Her arms are folded behind her back. Her breasts are framed, begging for my attention. My cock hardens.

"Do you write under your own name?" Stone asks.

The deep voice erases my vision. Thank fuck. I'm getting ready to masturbate at the breakfast table. What is wrong with me? I have to finish eating and get out of here—away from her.

"Pen name."

"What is it? Maybe I've read some of your books." Amy's excitement is adorable. "If I haven't, I'd love to."

Sonja glances up from whatever she'd been staring at on her plate. "I don't tell anyone my pen name once they know my real name. It's the only way I can keep my work separate from my personal life. You've met me as, uh, Sonja, but I prefer SJ. My agent used my...legal name. But since you know it, I wouldn't be comfortable if you knew my author name."

Did anyone else catch that hesitation? I scan the table, but there's no reaction beyond Stone nodding in approval. Yet another reason to stay away from her. I've played too many hands of poker in my life not to know a bluff when I see one. She's lying about her names or something. I'm sure of it.

"You said your editor or agent or whatever paid for you to stay in Colorado. Why not pay for you to take a trip for research?"

SJ shrugs.

"There's a club in Colorado Springs. I'd be willing to take you." Eliot smiles at her, and I want to punch that grin off his face.

"No. I'll take her." Did that just come out of my mouth? I press my lips together to keep more dumb ideas from spewing out. Eliot and his boys would turn SJ into their plaything. And his kink—their kink—is multiple partners. Their lack of expertise in bondage, in discipline, doesn't explain my stupid outburst.

Blue eyes blink up at me. Her rosebud lips form a perfect O. "You will?"

My dick short circuits imagining what I could do with that mouth.

"Road trip," Stone states. "We'll all go. We can check on Blake while we're there."

And with that proclamation, I'm screwed. No matter how I promise myself I won't get tangled in this woman's web of lies—once we get inside Pandora, it will take everything in me to keep my hands *and* my ropes off her.

FOUR

SJ

I can't believe I told them I write BDSM. Where did that come from? The conversation with my uncle. And the discussion I overheard last night while they were having dinner. Some small part of me must have still been wondering why Alex tied up my cousin. A fetish would explain it. That same small part of me doesn't want *this* Alex to be *that* Alex. And if he is, there has to be a reason. My uncle doesn't believe there's a reasonable explanation. Maybe I should leave now. Retreat to my apartment outside of Dallas and give up ever writing a book.

A firm knock at the door to my room startles me from my place at the window. It can't be Alex. He practically ran out of the inn after it was decided we were going to a club. I open up to find Tyler standing ramrod straight on the other side, green eyes boring into me as if he can see all my sins. The hair on the back of my neck stands up. Has he figured out I'm about to ruin Alex's life?

"If you want to go to the club, we have to give them your information for a background check."

I step back in silent invitation. No way I'm doing this in the hallway. "You know I'm staying here under an alias."

He nods and closes the door behind him but doesn't move into the room.

"If I give you my real name, how many people will it be shared with?" I'm wringing my hands, a total tell. I force them to still. Why the hell did my uncle register me under a fake name? Another layer of complication I don't need.

"I spent my career as an FBI agent. I can keep your real identity a secret. Only our contact at the club will know, and I'll explain the sensitivity of the information." How is this guy, who looks like an aging—in a good way—surfer able to project such an air of authority?

I clear my throat. "Sarah Jane Reading. That's R-E-A-D-I-N-G."

"Driver's license?"

Right. He'll need all my info. I hesitate. If Alex has shared his past with Tyler—if he's *the* Alex my uncle is searching for—my Texas ID could give it all away.

"I'll call from the office phone and bring it right back."

My uncle's voice echoes through my head, "I think you might owe me, don't you?" But really, if I do this, it's for my cousin, whom I love. I dig out the card proving my real identity from a zippered pocket in my bag. I hesitate as I'm about to hand it over. Tyler's eyes have softened, and he holds out an open palm. I take a shaky breath and place the card in his hand. "Guard this with your life."

"Did Amy tell you that she used to be in witness protection? Probably not. I was her handler and kept all her secrets. Trained her to keep them too. You can trust me."

Sweet, innkeeper Amy was in WitSec? I bet *that's* a story.

"I'll bring it right back." He's gone before I can undo my decision.

I close my eyes and pray this doesn't bite me in the ass. Then it hits me. I'm going to a BDSM club, and I don't know the first thing about them. I grab my phone and start searching for books. *The Bonds of Love* by Cecilia Tan. Looks good. I add it to my e-library and keep searching. Marie Tuhart. Raisa Greywood. After adding more books than I can possibly read, I search for the club.

Pandora has a quirky welcoming website. Nothing that screams black-leather, ass-beating scary bastards.

I roll my eyes at myself. Clearly I have some preconceived notions I need to get over. The site lists educational webinars, potluck lunches, and movie night. I half expect them to have daycare hours for the kids. Maybe they do—I giggle. I close the browser on my phone—enough playing on the internet.

If this Alex is who my uncle is looking for, if I'm

going to pull off getting him to confess what he did or possibly replicate it with me. A shiver shoots up my spine. I'll have to get real comfortable real quick with being tied up and losing all control. My throat tightens, and I gasp for breath. No matter what, if he tries to force his dick in my mouth, I'll bite it off. No matter how attractive he is, that's one thing I just can't... I wouldn't be able to stop myself.

I shake off the hideous memories bubbling up. *Breathe.*

One thing at a time. *Breathe.*

First, I have some reading to do. *Breathe.*

Tyler returns my ID as I'm about to settle into my first book. "All set."

First hurdle cleared.

Two days later, I've read several books, rubbed out several orgasms, and I'm hopelessly intrigued. All the stories focus heavily on consent, on the emotional connection, the changes in mental state that the partners experience in a scene. I can't deny how sexy the power dynamics are, and I'm curious.

Eliot's van is huge and has an electric lift at the back for a wheelchair. Not sure what that's for, but I don't ask. A short way into the long drive to Colorado Springs, Stone, in the front passenger seat, asks Eliot what's going on with Blake's recovery. I lean forward from the last row. Amy's beside Tyler in the second row, and Alex is leaning as far away from me as he can, despite the fact we're sharing the bench seat.

Eliot doesn't take his eyes from the road or lift a finger

from the steering wheel. "Physically, he's making good progress. Graci found a reflexologist couple in Albuquerque who have worked with stroke victims, paraplegics, and even quads. They've been advising her on Zoom, and they agreed to drive up for a weekend intensive and work with her on techniques."

"That's good news." Stone's deep voice resonates with hope.

"Graci said she's seen Blake move his other foot when she's working on him."

"What does Blake say?" Alex asks.

Eliot shrugs. "Ask him when you see him."

A heavy emotional fog coats the interior of the van, weighing down any further conversation for miles. I try to piece together what I know of Eliot and what I've heard of Blake, but I don't have enough to form the barest sketch. And it's clear this is not a topic that invites the questions of strangers. Alex is avoiding looking at me, much less speaking. I pull up one of my research books on my phone and try to mentally prepare for my club visit. The characters in the story are discussing the scene they will share. The safe words, the limits.

Hours later, we hit traffic, and I assume we're either close to or in Colorado Springs. Eliot's phone rings a number over the vehicle speakers.

"Hey, El."

"Cade," Eliot responds to the man who answered. "We're getting into town now. Where are you?"

"PT." This Cade person sounds defeated, and my heart aches for him.

"How much longer?"

"Just got here, so couple hours."

"We'll head there first."

The call ends without further discussion or even goodbyes. No one says a word. The mood is so heavy, it doesn't feel right to keep reading sexy stories. I'm not sure I should be going wherever the van is headed, but I can't demand they drop me off, no matter how much I'm dreading what might happen next.

Eliot parks the van in front of what looks like the main clubhouse for luxury apartments. His hands are still wrapped around the steering wheel. He puts his head down for a moment and sighs like he's praying for strength. Whatever is in that building is a tragic story I'm not ready to hear.

Everyone piles out with a few groans and some impromptu stretching. Alex moves as if he was merely on the couch for an episode of his favorite show. No moans, no stretching. The third row was fine, but even I drop forward and slowly roll out my spine once I'm outside. When I'm upright again, he has his back to me. "Coming or what?"

"I can stay with the van." I don't belong in the middle of whatever is happening here.

Amy comes up and hooks my elbow. "It's too hot out here. Come inside."

An elderly woman with a wash-and-set hairdo lifts her chin when the sliding glass doors open. A warm smile brightens her face, and she stands to come out from behind the curved faux-wood reception desk. She opens her arms wide. "Eliot."

He bends in half to return the hug, wrapping the small woman in his bare, dark arms. His short-sleeved blue shirt stretches across his back. "Miss Angie."

Oh gosh. We're at the reception desk, and already I'm having all kinds of gooey emotions.

Eliot stands to full height, his hands in Angie's. "How's he doing?"

Everyone else is signing in to a guest book on the top of the reception desk. Amy hands me the pen. "They have to log visitors for insurance or something."

I sign in as SJ and a scribble for my last name. And then I'm moving with the group down a large bead board hallway dotted by occasional clusters of two chairs and a small end table. Framed artwork dots the length of the walls, and a glass cabinet holds flyers and a calendar of events. We pass a huge dining room set with round wood tables for four with small vases of daisies. The decor is warm, upscale lodge or resort. But there is evidence of the institutional nature of the place in the tiny details— wheels on the chairs and tables and the people in white scrubs who are cleaning up after the midday meal.

Eliot leads us onto an elevator big enough to hold a hospital bed or two. We drop one floor to a basement level. The doors open to a space that's more clinical, less art and furniture, but still inviting with warm paint and wood accents. After a few twists and turns, we arrive at another set of glass doors. They part, and the sounds of what I assume is a gym waft out. Grunts. Coaches encouraging. But once past the partition, I see this isn't an ordinary gym. It's a physical therapy space, based on the mats on the floor, the parallel bars for assisted walking, the walls of equipment, and the wheelchairs both with and without occupants. There are only four clusters of people in the cavernous space.

Eliot is moving full-speed to where a beautiful blond man is lying on a mat while a woman with long dark hair pulled into a ponytail is stretching his pitifully thin, scarred leg. Two other men stand by, their features etched with concern. Eliot's back is to us, and I can't hear what he says, but the woman stands and gives him a warm hug that lasts longer than I would expect for a professional relationship. The olive-skinned man with short dark hair is moving toward us. Tyler meets him a few feet before he reaches us. "Pierce. How's he doing?"

Pierce scrubs his hair back. "Hard to say. His upper body is strong, but there's still not much from the waist down. Although, he's off the catheter as of a couple days ago."

"That's huge." Tyler looks back to Amy and tugs her forward into his embrace like he needs to hold someone.

Pierce grimaces. "Tell that to Blake."

Alex ignores our gathering, going to Blake. He drops to the mat on his knees and puts a hand on Blake's shoulder. "Hey, buddy. Looking good."

"You talking to me or Graci?"

Alex grins. "Good to see you again, Graci. When am I busting my friend here outta this place?"

Graci, the physical therapist, shifts to Blake's other

leg. "That's up to this guy." She smiles at Blake and shifts his leg back a bit farther. Blake groans. "He's kind of grumpy about my workouts."

"She's trying to kill me."

"Dude. You're complaining about a beautiful woman at your feet, massaging your legs?" Alex nudges Graci's shoulder with his. "Where can I sign up for this kind of abuse?"

"Sure, she looks nice now. In about two hours, she's gonna make sure I'm crying." Blake scowls at the woman. "My favorite part is when she tells me to walk."

The other man standing watch, younger, with big soft brown eyes, his arms crossed, chirps, "That's because you will walk again."

"Cade," Blake says with an exasperated tone. He shifts his attention to Eliot. "So what are you doing here? Going to the club?"

Eliot nods. "That's the plan."

"Good, take this one with you. He's driving me nuts." Blake hitches his thumb in Cade's direction. "Get him laid."

Cade barks out a pained sound of protest. Eliot is flicking his gaze between them.

"I'm not going to a club without you." Cade crosses his arms and looks like he's about to cry.

"I don't need a goddamned keeper. Go to the fucking club, Cade." Blake closes his eyes, and his hands ball into fists.

Graci adjusts Blake's leg, deepening the stretch. "I'll be around tonight. There's an *Almost Human* marathon starting this afternoon. They're showing them in the correct chronological order. Will you be my geek TV buddy?"

"I don't need a pity party," Blake answers.

"Hey, now you're in for it. We're walking for sure today." Her voice has a bit of an edge and an accent.

"Are you ever going to let anyone in again?" Cade demands.

Alex rises and puts his arm around Cade. "Hey, how about we take a break? Get a cold drink. Graci isn't going to let him run away."

Cade lets Alex lead him away. Graci's gaze follows them long enough for me to see the longing in her gaze. For Alex? Or Cade? She returns her focus to Blake before I can decide.

I don't know the whole story, but the tension that filled this huge space releases. Alex has his head close to Cade's. What could he possibly be telling the man? He's clearly distraught by Blake's situation. More than Pierce. Even more than Eliot, who stands beside him but has his hands in his pockets, a relaxed stance, taking in the work happening. "Graci, you just want to see your show on the big TV we put in Blake's room."

"Of course that's it, Eliot. Not this guy's super friendly personality." She sticks her tongue out at Blake and keeps working.

"Heard you had some movement during reflexology." Stone glares down at Blake.

Blake shifts his gaze away, not answering. From what I've seen, he's the only one who defies Stone.

"I've been working his feet daily. Did a Zoom session with the pros. They're trying to figure out their schedule to do in-person sessions."

"Bunch of woo woo bullshit." Blake directs his spite at Graci, who doesn't react at all.

"Did your foot move or not?" Stone's a judge demanding the truth.

"Yes." Blake barely lets the word out, clearly resenting the forced admission.

If I were him, I'd be doing whatever I could to get movement back. Woo woo or not. Graci's a saint to put up with his grumpy ass. Or well paid.

Amy, Tyler, and Stone shift closer to each other and start a murmured conversation. I back away from what is clearly a family moment, stepping out of the room. In the hallway, I spy Alex holding a sobbing Cade. He's rubbing the man's back and telling him things will get better. Each change so far has been an improvement. That Cade has to be patient with Blake. My heart squeezes.

There's no way this can be the Alex my uncle is looking for, right? I escape to the women's restroom and try to reconcile the criminal image my uncle painted with this caring version of Alex.

There is something so compelling about a man who will hold another man, care for him emotionally. Especially when the man is a strapping cowboy who works construction. Like he isn't attractive enough, he has to show this sensitive side?

I don't want him to be Alex Craig, the man who hurt my cousin.

I'm washing my hands when Amy enters the restroom. "There you are."

I smile into the mirror at her and try to create a reasonable excuse for making myself scarce.

"It can be a lot. It's easier now that he isn't confined to the hospital bed, hooked to all kinds of wires."

I shudder at the image. "What happened to him?"

"Short version. Car accident. He nearly didn't make it."

"He looks good for having almost died."

"Getting better each day. But it's hard on his partners."

Partners is a loaded word, one Amy used intentionally. One that sort of explains some of the tension between Blake and Cade.

"Anyway, if you're done, we're going to book some hotel rooms, now that we have a plan. Eliot's coming to the club, but he's staying with Cade at the rental house here in town. We need to get a room count."

I follow Amy out the door to find all the guys in the hallway.

Stone is speaking to Pierce. "If you're willing to rideshare with Eliot back to the house, I can drive everyone else in the van. We need a room for me, one for Amy and Tyler—"

"I can share," I say. "No big deal if we get a room with two beds."

Alex crosses his arms. "I'll pay for two rooms."

Stone finishes as if we haven't spoken. "Four rooms. I'll check with the hotel we used last time."

Ouch.

Does Alex think I'm going to jump him? Well, that's not completely out of bounds. The urge to climb him like a tree and talk about what to do with his wood has been riding me since I saw him. But it's not like I could take advantage of him. Except, he might try something with me. No. No way. Not possible.

FIVE

ALEX

I rub the back of my neck. I could have handled the hotel room thing better, but no way am I sharing with some random chick from Texas. Especially one as sexy as SJ is and one who focuses so hard on me. I swear I don't make a move without her eyes on me. But that's no excuse for being rude.

"Sit up here with Amy. Pierce and I can take the back row." I hold out my hand to help her in. She hesitates, and it kills me. I obviously hurt her feelings. Her fingers are chilled when she finally grabs my hand. I'm tempted to chafe them between my palms to warm her up. But I release her and climb in behind.

Check-in is smooth, but we have a few hours before the club will open. I'd be fine watching TV and chilling out, but Stone orders us to show up for dinner. I swear, only my mama was as big a stickler for family dinners. A pang of longing careens through me, leaving a shredded ache. I haven't been at my family's dinner table in almost ten years. Amy and the guys are great, but they're no substitute. I'm ashamed by my disloyalty to the people who have "found" me and provided as close to a family as possible. But I didn't lose my family. They didn't abandon me. I had to leave because of my own stupid choices.

Going to the club is less and less appealing. I gotta get my head out of my ass.

Dinner, a shower, and a short nap help. I'm something close to human when we climb into the van again. Cade and Eliot pack in with us when we stop by their rental house. This giant van that seemed like overkill when there were six of us riding in it shrinks to the size of a clown car. If clowns wore black leather and micro-mini skirts. Amy is sitting on Tyler's lap. Not exactly kosher, but Eliot is the safest driver I know and we're only a few blocks from the club. I wouldn't mind having SJ on my lap. She must have borrowed one of Amy's outfits, because, damn. Her legs are a mile long, and her ass is stretching the shiny black fabric that barely covers her in a way that brings tears to a man's eyes and steel to his dick.

The van is quiet enough that Tyler's whispered promises are nearly understandable. The sexual tension is off the charts. The only one who appears unaffected is Stone. But that man's feathers don't ruffle. I'm pretty sure he could be in the middle of a tornado, and it would veer to avoid him. I'm itchy to open my bag and check my equipment. The gear I keep in perfect condition. The carabiners clipped together by size. The rings in their own separate zipper pouch. The hanks I formed and sorted hours before we left the Sunflower. I rub my hands down my black jeans to ease the obsessive urge.

Pierce still works part-time at Pandora, so he takes the lead on getting us into the club, chatting with the guy at the front. Each of us rattle off our names, Amy Davis, Tyler Davis.

"Alex Craig." I point to my name on his members list and flash my ID as I move inside.

Eliot Hughes, Cade Ramos, Stone. The guys rattle off their names as they file past me.

SJ is the only nonmember guest, so she has to sign the agreement to follow the rules. Her hand shakes a little as she initials each one—probably nervous about her first experience in a dungeon.

"We'll meet you down there," Eliot says. Cade and Pierce follow him to the elevator.

After SJ finishes with her form, the ladies visit the locker room. Tyler, Stone, and I wait in the hallway, the anticipation building and keeping us silent. We left everything at the hotel room, except for the tool bags Tyler and I carry.

Finally we're moving down the wide hallway to the freight-sized elevator that will lower us into the Box. The thumping music hits low in my gut. I glance at SJ. The beat isn't waking her up so much as rattling her bones. I'm pretty sure she's feeling like a nervous hound in a thunderstorm. My hand twitches to reach out, but I hold back. As soon as the door slides open and the dark, cavernous space is exposed, Tyler grabs Amy's hand and leads her directly to the spanking bench. Stone beelines for the table where Pierce, Cade, and Eliot are already chatting up a couple of women. This should be interesting.

SJ hasn't moved. My plan to let one of the others show her around isn't going to work. I grit my teeth. "Can I give you the nickel tour?"

She whooshes out a breath and nods at me. I offer my hand, and she hesitates before taking it. Her fingers were chilled before; now they're ice cubes. We're at the damn door, and she's losing her shit. I'm tempted to turn around and send her back to the hotel, but she steps off the elevator and turns to the right. "Show me everything."

Little spitfire's got grit, I'll give her that.

I lead her to the St. Andrew's cross. A Domme is having fun with a naked male subbie who is bound facing the room but wearing a blindfold. She walks around him, checking his bindings, dragging her fingers lightly over his armpits and other vulnerable spots. It's a wicked show of dominance without impact. She works him over with a feather wand, flitting randomly from spot to spot and occasionally lingering until her boy is twitching and begging. Based on his cock, he's loving everything she's giving him. She will probably move on to more intense sensations, but she has her sub's entire attention right now. Exactly why I love my ropes.

I check our table. Stone is alone with one of the women who had been chatting with Eliot and the guys. Maybe she'd be willing to finish giving SJ the tour. I lead her toward the table. Stone waves us over when we're still feet away. As soon as we reach them, Stone introduces the girl—she must be barely old enough to be at the club —as Cassie.

"Ma'am," I say automatically. And I introduce SJ.

"Nice to meet you." Cassie smiles, but it's clear she's nervous. Stone puffs up as if he needs to protect her from us. What's that about?

When SJ doesn't jump in, the conversation dies. My sister or my mother would have already been pulling out the chair nearest Cassie and asking intrusive questions. Cassie seems enthralled with Stone, and SJ's focus is still flitting around the club. I set my bag on an empty chair, and rather than stand around awkwardly, I ask, "Ready to check out some more?"

SJ blinks up at me as if she forgot I'm here. "Sure."

Over at one of the spanking benches, Tyler ties Amy in place. "Want to see some impact play? Tyler and Amy are about to scene."

I take SJ by the shoulder and pivot her to face the right direction. Tyler lifts Amy's skirt to bare her ass and delivers a warmup smack. SJ jerks in my grip.

"Um. Maybe not." Her cheeks pinken, and she turns her head away.

Interesting. I lean close to her ear and whisper, "Is it because you know them, or is it the spanking? Does his hand on her ass make your pussy wet?"

Her blush deepens to match the red of her hair. She turns, and her lips are nearly on mine. "Did you just ask me about my pussy?"

Damn. I did. I shouldn't, but I really want her to answer. I let the fire I'm feeling burn in my gaze. "Yes."

Her mouth forms a perfect O and her eyes widen. My cock loves that reaction.

Let's see what else gets her going.

I grab her hand and head directly for the rigging stage. A couple I've seen before has the stage. Perfect. She's a former dancer, ballet or something, and flexible as all hell. Her partner, lithe as she is and slightly older, moves around her, embracing her with his entire body as he weaves and knots his ropes. They're beautiful to watch but not at all instructional. His rigging appears like magic around her. I'm envious of the years they've had to work together to be so in sync that they look as natural as a flower blooming. That kind of partnership doesn't happen with a single hookup—the only kind of play I let myself have.

With SJ directly in front of me, it's easy to talk without disturbing the scene. "What do you think?"

Her breath puffs out in a subtle pant. Her fingers warm in my light hold. Her body shifts as if the ropes are tugging her forward as her breasts are framed. Damn. She's into it. My cock twitches with need, and my urge to get out my gear comes roaring back.

I lean closer, close enough to smell the light fruity scent of her hair. "You like what you see."

She nods in the barest acknowledgement.

As we stand there, she leans into me, her back resting against my chest. I should shift away, but I can't. Finally, the couple wraps up their scene with the woman spinning slightly above the floor in a beautifully balanced suspension.

With SJ's vibrant red hair and curvy body, she would be stunning floating in air, naked, my ropes pinning her place. My fingers digging into her hips as my dick slides in and out of her luscious body. My cock lengthens uncomfortably behind my zipper. *Whoa.* I step back.

"Ready?" I have to clear my throat of the lingering effects of my fantasy.

SJ follows toward the middle of the club and taps me on the shoulder.

I stop.

"How did he know how to tie all those knots and how many times to wrap the rope around her body? How did he get the knots to lie so flat? Does the rope scratch her skin?"

Holy shit. She's fascinated. I consider going back to the table, grabbing my gear, and showing her the answers. Up close. In person. No. She doesn't have a clue and can't consent. And I don't need to start something with someone I'm living with, even if it is in separate rooms.

I swallow down my perverted desires and try to answer with as little emotion as possible. "He's likely been practicing for years. Probably taken classes or gone to conferences to learn. You can tell they've been together as a couple for a long time. There's an artistry to that kind of rope play."

"Obviously. It was beautiful the way she trusted him and he took care of her while he restrained her. But it wasn't totally about that, was it?"

"What?"

"Restraint. Control. Domination."

"It is, on some level, absolutely about all that." I don't want to lie to her and let her believe that the dominance isn't a huge draw. "But part of dominance is care. The reason she trusts him is she knows she can release all control to him and he'll care for her. They're beautiful together because of that trust." Trust I thought I'd found so early in my exploration. Trust that had been completely violated. "It's just as important for the Dom to trust his sub. The suspension they did, he had to trust that if something felt...off, she would tell him. Those two are so tight together, they're communicating without words. Her shift of an arm or tilt of her head had him readjusting, responding to what her body needed. That's why they're so captivating."

"When she lifted off the ground... I didn't expect that. It was breathtaking."

Damn, she did see the artistry.

"How does that even work? Ropes and some metal clips, and her entire body was suspended."

"There's a fair amount of physics and some anatomy involved. Tying someone, bondage, is one level. They're at a completely different level. Shibari."

"What do you do? Bondage or art?" Her blue eyes bore into me, searching for my secrets.

"I can do either. Depends on my partner."

"What would you do with me?" She blinks her pretty eyes, gaze soft and inviting.

Fuck. Her question might as well be her hand

wrapped around my cock. I'd do everything with her. But I can't. "Nothing."

"What?" She stiffens.

"I have to go." I grab her hand and tug her to where Stone is sitting with Cassie. Tyler and Amy have rejoined them, Amy's on Tyler's lap, cuddled close. As soon as we're within range, I say, "I'm going back to the hotel. Not feeling well." I drop SJ's hand and pick up my bag. Before anyone can argue with me, I'm in the elevator sucking in air and praying my cock will settle down on its own. It won't. Image after image of all the ways I could tie SJ up flash before my eyes like an old-fashioned slide show of vacation pictures. Click. SJ, arms folded behind her, bare breasts wrapped and framed with a center knot. Click. SJ suspended, cradled with her thighs tied to her arms, open completely. Wet and dripping. Begging me to fuck her. Click.

The elevator door opens, and I shake the images from my bastard brain. I don't retrieve my phone until I'm outside sucking in the cool night air. The rideshare shows up, and within minutes I'm back at the hotel.

I drop my gear and strip. The shower offers no relief. With a soaped-up hand, I stroke away my longing. Only it doesn't get washed away with my cum around the drain. Instead it builds. SJ with me under the water, the marks from my ropes still visible on her skin. Her hands on me. My tongue dancing with hers. Her hair in my fist as I press her against the tile wall and fuck her until neither of us can move.

I slam the water off, grab a towel, and barely dry off

before I'm laid out naked on the bed, lube on the nightstand ready to help me abuse myself with images of what can never be until I finally pass out.

The sound of an injured animal has me jolting awake. What the fuck was that? I'm up and searching for the source before I'm fully aware. The connecting door. I open my side. Press my ear to the door to Sonja's room.

"I'm doing the best I can." The pain in her high-pitched voice stabs me through the thick door. I press my palm to it as if I could comfort her.

"This isn't what we agreed to." Is she crying?

That's it. I knock on the door, three firm raps. "SJ."

She mumbles something.

I knock again harder.

The lock clicks, she opens the door, and she's still dressed in her club gear.

"Are you okay?" I ask, reaching out to swipe away a tear.

"Are you naked?"

Aw shit. I drop my hands and cover my junk. "I was asleep. Sounded like you were in trouble. I wasn't... I shouldn't..."

"My agent's upset."

"He shouldn't talk to you like that." Because it's lighting up all kinds of protective instincts in me.

"You could hear him?" She clasps her arms protectively.

"No, I could hear *you*. Maybe you need a new agent."

"It's not that simple. I'm...late. On my book."

I reach up and stroke the hair back from her face.

"No matter how late you are, it's not okay for someone to abuse you." I'm sure not going to let her be bullied over a book contract. Not right under my nose. "If you ever want me to tie you up for real, you'll have to learn to say no and mean it. Even when you're not in the obvious position of power, you still have to be assertive when it comes to your safety, your mental health, your well-being."

Somehow SJ is in my arms. She trails her fingers down my cheek, and I tilt my head down to kiss her. Her lips touch mine, and electricity flows from my mouth directly to my balls. I press my hips forward into the cradle of her thighs. She grips my biceps and steps back. She swipes her lips with her tongue, and my knees shake with need.

"I can't do this." She takes another step back, and I mirror her movement because she's right. "Not with you. Not tonight."

The next thing I know, the lock on her door is snicking into place.

How did that happen? What is it about this woman?

I haven't been alone and naked with a woman anywhere in almost ten years, much less a hotel room. The image of SJ screaming for help and my life imploding again is enough to kill any lingering lust and deflate my dick. But my gut is still demanding I protect her from the asshole on the other end of the phone. My guts will have to shut the hell up, because it's not my place to deal with her agent, even if he is making her act like a victim. She's not my problem.

The alarm goes off before I've had a wink of sleep, at least not any actual rest. Images of SJ in my rigging warred with images of her being taken away by a shadow of a monster. I fucked and fought in my dreams the rest of the night, but we have to check out. I grab a shower and head downstairs to meet the group. After a quick bite of breakfast at the hotel buffet, we're loaded back in the van. Stone's driving. Tyler shotgun. I'm in the last row behind Amy and SJ. Guess Eliot decided to stay and spend time with Blake. I tilt my head back and close my eyes, intending to get the rest I missed while I was sleeping.

"How'd you get started writing BDSM romance, SJ?" Stone's question, lobbed into the back seat, has me jolting up.

She laughs nervously. Stone has that effect on people. The van is silent, waiting for her to answer. Guess we're all curious.

"Well." She tilts her head and straightens. "I started in copywriting. Brochures, ad copy, rebranding. Stuff like that."

Stone's cold gaze in the rearview mirror makes me want to confess everything, and I'm not even the one being grilled.

"But the writing I was doing for work was pretty boring. There's only so many things that can be said about oatmeal and diapers. Right?"

"Why BDSM?"

"It was a good niche. Popular. And I like reading those books."

I wait for what Stone will reply. Will he tell her she

has no business writing about a community she doesn't know the first thing about? Will he give her approval for following her dreams?

Stone's not done. "Do you like writing about BDSM?"

"Yes?" The interrogation is starting make Sonja nervous.

"Would you be interested in a little cross-over job? Copywriting and BDSM?"

She bites her lip. "Maybe? What would it involve?"

A job? Stone's offering her a job. What the hell?

"We have a website person creating our site for our new club. But she needs help with the content, and none of us has the time or the skill to get the wording right. I'd also like some internal documents, like brochures."

Brochures? What is Stone gonna do, pass them out at the next Commerce meeting? Or maybe ask the Alabaster innkeepers to post them in their B and B's?

"That sounds interesting, but I usually have a point of contact for my product descriptions."

I suddenly see where this is going. "Don't you need to work on your book? You're already behind."

Stone's glare through the rearview mirror is impossible to ignore.

"Actually, it might be exactly what I need to get over my writer's block. Something else to focus on but still on topic. Might even prime the pump." She shrugs and gives me a smile over her shoulder.

"Perfect. We'll work out the details on the pay and due dates when we get back to the Sunflower. Alex will be your subject matter expert. You can show her the ropes, can't you, Alex?"

Stone backed me into the corner perfectly, and there's not a damn thing I can do. His steely gaze dares me to try. I could argue that I'm too busy with the construction, but he'll call it out as the lame excuse it is. I'd settle this like I used to with my buddies back in Texas, a good punch to the gut, but Stone probably knows six ways to kill me before breakfast and could make my body disappear for good measure.

I nod while the voice in my head screams nope.

SIX

SJ

It's been almost two weeks, and I've barely seen Alex. He's out in the morning before anyone else wakes up for breakfast. From what I understand, he's working his ass off to get the club ready. Ever since I heard him say his name at Pandora, I've been struggling to believe that the hard-working, super-polite man I'm living with, who has so many friends who trust him, hurt my cousin. He's nothing like the men who convinced me I'd be a model.

I avoid thinking about Alex and my uncle by doing a ton of research on BDSM, specifically bondage. I keep coming back to the beautiful images of Shibari. The intricate wraps and perfectly aligned knots. There is such symmetry and artistry in the pictures. Some of the more typical BDSM bondage is a little rough for me, but the Shibari is intriguing. No matter how much I've searched, the couple at Pandora are unmatched in any videos I've found. Each day I add to the notes in my notebook, filling it with as many questions as facts. I even started toying with the idea of using it in my book.

Finally, I find Amy in the dining room after everyone has left for the day.

"You're still here?" I ask.

She sets her coffee cup on the coaster. "I'm so sorry. I've been such a bad host. The guys have me busy picking paint colors and fabric and artwork for the guest suites and all the public spaces for the resort. This construction project has taken over our lives."

I sit down across from her. "Please don't apologize. I've been making some progress on my book." At least I'm not lying. "And I started work on the copy for the website. But the best stories are personal. What's the origin story of the club or resort? How did all of you get invested in this project? How'd you even meet? You're all so different."

"We met through the club we belonged to back in Missouri."

"Is that where you met Tyler? He said something about you being in witness protection?"

"The two are related. I had a terrible work situation— literally the boss from hell."

Boss from hell. That's what my uncle is becoming. Convinced me he had only my interests, my future in mind when he gifted me this writing retreat. Now I'm helping him track a fugitive.

Amy twists her teacup on the coaster. "I was looking

for an emotional release for my anxiety. No strings attached." She lifts her chin, and her gaze is assessing. "Something about impact play allows me to let go of all the details, the future worries, the churning of possibilities in my head. I was desperate when I visited the club." Her face softens, and her eyes are dreamy and soft. Even her shoulders drop to a more relaxed position. "And I met Tyler."

It's clear how much she loves him from that change in expression alone.

"It's easy in my head to write a book with these kinds of relationships." I laugh through my nervousness. "Happily ever after—the end. But I don't think about what comes next in real life. Do you scene at home?"

Her cheeks pinken and she drops her gaze to her cup. Amy's brown eyes are twinkling as she faces me again. "Are you asking me if Tyler spanks me outside the club?"

"Not if you don't want me to." I twist a lock of my hair around my finger. As soon as I realize I'm doing it, I stop and unwind my finger. This conversation is making me nervous too. "But...why go to a club if you can express yourself at home?"

"Everyone's reasons and ways to express their sexuality are different. For Tyler and me, we occasionally like to express ourselves in a more public place like the club. At first, the club was safety. There were dungeon monitors and other members I could rely on to make sure my boundaries were respected. In a private setting, the possibility for abuse, especially from someone you don't know well, is higher. At least that was my reasoning. Luckily, I met Tyler on my first visit. Like it was meant to be."

"You said 'at first'. Why do you continue to visit?"

Amy smiles, and a titter of a laugh escapes her. "Tyler likes to show me off, and I like the possessiveness it triggers in him. There's also something incredibly erotic for me to have witnesses to my submission. I guess I'm a closet exhibitionist. Or maybe a club one."

"I can see that." The couple who were dancing with the ropes were definitely putting on a performance but in an intimate headspace. It made sense they would be in the club because of the support needed to do suspension. But it must be possible to create a structure at home. Maybe they rent.

"There's also the sense of community. It's nice to not be the only one in a room full of people with a kink. At the club, everyone in the room has one." Amy shrugs and sips her tea.

If I didn't know about her and Tyler, I wouldn't have guessed. She's such a girl-next-door, blend-in-with-the-crowd type, with her soft brown hair and matching eyes. She dresses like every other person I've seen in Colorado. Jeans. Comfortable shoes. Standard outdoorsy lifestyle they sell in clothing catalogs. What the outside world sees doesn't always tell the real story. Maybe it never does.

Maybe whatever my uncle saw isn't the whole story of what happened to my cousin.

If Alex did "ruin" Alyss, he's a horrible person. I wish I could see it. But all I've seen of Alex so far is a hard-working man who treats me with respect when he deals with me at all. Even when he was at the hotel room door naked, he was concerned for me, a stranger. As nice as it was to have him check on me, I'd rather that incident hadn't happened. I can't get the image out of my head. The man is cut like a warrior, solid like a statue, and two hands didn't cover him completely at all. Even now, my body is twitchy with the need to ride that man like a trick pony at the rodeo. Take him through all his paces and see what he can do. I'm pretty sure he'd ruin me. And my uncle would kill me. And if Alyss found out I was drooling over the man who'd hurt her—I'm the worst kind of cousin and friend.

How do I get to the truth?

I've got to figure out a way to get Alex to open up to me. Stone told Alex to help me with the marketing for the club. Tonight, I'll wait up for him. Maybe wear something tempting. Anything to get his attention.

I stand up, ready to leave, and realize I've been ignoring Amy. "I'm sorry. You gave me so much to think about, and I'm feeling the muse for my book."

She waves me off. "Go write. That's what you're here to do. I'm glad I could help."

I dart up the stairs and take a few minutes that turns into a few hours of writing. Ideas are flowing, for the book I came here to write and even some stuff for the club. I scour the internet for places real people are talking about their experience, but nothing beats seeing the club in person and talking to Amy in person.

I check the time. Well past noon. Last thing I ate was breakfast, and now that I focus on food, I'm starving.

Eliot and Cade are still in Colorado Springs. And Stone hasn't instigated a cookout in days. Instead of scrounging for something from Amy or waiting around until she invites me to join her and Tyler, I drive into the center of town. It's crowded with tourists—the overflow from Aspen I assume. Alabaster is a cute little mountain town with brick walkways and historic building storefronts. Flowing through the middle of town is a river that's supposed to be great for fishing. A few yards up the road, some picnic tables fill in the gap between the two-lane road and the sidewalk. When I'm close enough, I can see the sign: *Stone Bear Pub*. A waiter pops out the door in front of me, his arms loaded with waters. He plops them down in front of a family, even has a bowl of water for their dog. This place is the perfect spot for some people watching and a meal. I sit at the smaller round table with an umbrella. Maybe I should find a seat inside at the bar instead of taking an entire table to myself, but I want to be out and pretend for an hour or so that my life isn't fucked up. That my uncle isn't turning me into a spy, and that I don't have any doubts about what he accused Alex of doing. Because if my uncle is wrong...

"Hi, I'm Vince. I'll be taking care of you. Something to drink?" He sets a laminated two-sided menu in front of me.

"Iced tea?"

"Great. I'll be right back."

Everything the menu describes sounds delicious, and I'm trying to decide between a wood-fired pizza, a buffalo burger, or a plate of fish tacos, when a shadow passes over me.

"SJ?"

I jump in my chair, and it tilts.

Before I fall, Alex is there, holding me up. "Didn't mean to startle you."

"What are you doing here?" *Besides blocking out the sun and looking more delicious than anything on the menu?*

"Volunteered to get lunch for Gabe and me."

"That's nice of you." Again with the kind, considerate action that makes my uncle's story hard to believe.

"Not really." He chuckles self-consciously.

"I was just about to order. You could join me." I should probably be demanding he join me so I can ask him a ton of questions for the marketing materials.

He checks his phone. "Sure, I've got time."

Our knees graze under the table when he sits down. The slightest connection, but my core reacts. I shift in my chair, and then the waiter appears, saving me from my own awkwardness. Alex orders a sandwich, and I get the fish tacos, despite wanting the pizza.

"How's the project going?" I ask to fill the silence after the waiter leaves.

"It's good. The subcontractors have been great. Working with Gabe is perfect." He shrugs. "Biggest challenge will be getting everything done before winter weather hits."

I glance up at the perfectly blue sky and then give him a skeptical look.

"Weather can be murder on a construction timeline." His blue-gray eyes follow my every move. I try not to fidget.

"Sounds like the voice of experience. How long have you been doing construction?"

"Almost ten years. Started working with a cousin of mine. First, moving bags of concrete, carrying and cleaning tools, stuff like that until I built up my skills."

And his muscles. The man fills out his shirt. "Do you like it?"

"Most days. Today, not as much. Stone got this company to draw up the plans, and they're the primary contractor for the job. Unfortunately, the architect we're working with is...a lot."

"What do you mean?"

"She's the reason I volunteered to get lunch. Gabe doesn't mind her, but... It's me. I'm not used to being talked down to."

"Does Stone know?" I can't imagine Stone letting anyone treat any member of his "family" with less than total respect.

"She's kind of a carbon copy of Stone, but in stilettos instead of combat boots." He fiddles with the corner of the paper napkin.

"Oh." I finally get the picture. "Gabe's okay with her dominance."

Alex laughs and lifts his gaze to mine. "Yeah. He's probably used to it."

His face softens and lights up when he laughs, making him even more handsome. I can't look away from him, and his attention is addictive. I should ask him questions about his past, about Texas, or my cousin, but I can't think of anything that wouldn't ruin the moment. The waiter appears with our lunch, and Alex asks him to make a to-go order for Gabe. Before I know it, our plates are clean and he's putting money in the folder holding our check.

"Let me give you cash for mine," I say as he picks up Gabe's order.

"Nope. I don't get to have lunch with a pretty girl very often. It was my pleasure."

The way he says that last word sounds like a promise. "You'll have to let me return the favor while I'm here."

He tucks his chair in. "I might do that."

I return his teasing smile and shamelessly watch his backside as he walks away. The man is drool worthy. I drive back to the Sunflower no closer to a resolution as to who Alex is—the person I see, or the one my uncle claims he is.

Amy and Tyler are on the back porch sharing a meal, with eyes only for each other. I envy their life—quiet, committed, uncomplicated. From what Amy said, it hasn't always been like this for them, but it is now. And I want that too.

I try to write, but the words aren't flowing. An extended yoga session leaves me a bit sweaty, so I take my time with a luxurious bath in the claw foot tub. It's deep and the water seems to stay warm longer. After I shave everywhere, I coat my skin in lotion. Colorado is so dry. Hard to believe with all the green trees, but I can't keep myself or my skin hydrated. Finally, fatigue settles into my bones and I slip on barely there pajamas. It's nine thirty, and Alex still isn't back from work. The rest of the house is quiet. They get up so early that by ten, the place is shut down completely. I write out a list of questions for Alex to help me with the marketing material. At least I'll have done something. As I'm trying to think of more, my phone rings.

"Hi, Uncle." I try put some cheer in my voice, despite our last phone call. I'm pretty sure he was drunk.

"Why haven't you called? Did you find Alex Craig?"

I guess he doesn't remember our last call, since I already told him Alex is Alex Craig. I consider lying. Part of me wants to protect Alex, but I can't. "Yes. The Alex that lives here is named Alex Craig."

"I knew it."

"He's not a bad guy." I regret the words as soon as I say them.

He barks out a laugh filled with derision. "You wouldn't know a good man if Jesus himself asked you out."

Wow. I half expect to hear lightning strike.

"I paid for your plane ticket. I'm paying for that fancy hotel. You've got one job to do."

Write my book. "I'm working on it. I didn't say it would be easy or quick. It's not like I can snap my fingers and be done."

"All I'm asking is one small favor. Help me get Alex Craig."

What the heck does he mean? "What am I supposed to do?"

"We're family. You know what the word *family* means, girl? It means loyalty. It means protection. It means you doing whatever it takes to take care of each other."

He's right. When I was taken by the man who promised me a career of fame and instead used me like trash, my uncle is the one who rescued me. No questions asked. He used all the power he had to free me from a situation that would have killed me. I've been so caught up in learning about this BDSM stuff that I forgot about the truth. I hang my head.

My uncle saved me back then and now is paying for this writing retreat so I can safely chase my new dream. I owe him.

I resolve to do whatever he asks. "What do you need?"

"Find out where he's been and get some dirt on him that's current. People like him don't stop. What he did to Alyss, he's done to someone else. Get the proof." He hangs up without a goodbye.

If Alex is the predator my uncle thinks he is, then he's not a good man. But if I pursue him, everyone here, Alex's found family, will hate me, and they're so nice.

This situation would be so much simpler if they were like the photographers who took advantage of me. No different than people on the streets seducing young girls. I could seek a twisted version of revenge and have no guilt. But I can't because of the rules they discussed the first night I arrived.

And they're treating me so well.

But my uncle has a valid point. I owe it to my family to stop Alex.

But even as I try to convince myself this is the correct course of action, I falter. My life has been a series of bad decisions, so how can I know if the choice I'm making now is the right one?

SEVEN

ALEX

"Hey, brother."

I turn to face Gabe, freezing mid-swipe with my plaster. "S'up?"

"We're ahead of schedule. I say we knock off early." He's probably missing his wife, Katherine.

Unlike me, he doesn't have a reason to avoid going home. "You go ahead. I'm gonna finish this wall. I'll catch a rideshare."

"You sure? I can stay."

"No way. Katherine'll beat me if she finds out I kept you late on a Friday for no good reason."

"Don't pretend you wouldn't like it." Gabe nudges my shoulder. "All right. I'm outta here. Don't stay too late, or Larry won't be working."

The one rideshare driver in the area who will take me all the way back to Alabaster. "No worries. Like I said, just finishing this wall."

Except that I keep going. I finish the tape and texture for the entire room. As I'm cleaning my tools and trying to figure out how to get home or where to sleep onsite, headlights flash in the windows.

Stone comes sauntering in a few minutes later. He glances around the room. "Looks good. Ready?"

I dry my trowel and tuck it in my tool bag. With a nod, I follow Stone out, locking the doors behind us. I'd ask how he knew I was there, and without a car, but that would be wasted breath. Stone knows shit, and he doesn't reveal his sources. I'll ask Gabe on Monday.

We don't get back to the Sunflower until after midnight. I'm too tired to eat, but I could use a shower. Stone is already headed up the stairs, and I drag my ass up behind him. His bedroom door closes as I hit the landing. The hallway looks forever long, and I have to pass SJ's room. I've been working every hour there is to stay away from her and all her questions because each minute I'm near her is torture. I have to mentally and physically restrain myself from pursuing her. She's captivating. And delicate. And a risk to the barriers I've put in place to protect myself.

Her door is ajar. Unable to help myself, I peek in. She's curled in a ball on top of the covers, her phone by her hand. It's a protective position, but she's exposed, her top having ridden up to her ribs. An elaborate tattoo covers the small of her back—an elegant butterfly with a heart as its body, wearing a crown and surrounded by tendrils of flowers, vines, and leaves. The vines have captured the butterfly.

Does she realize what this says?

Does it mean the same thing to her?

Or was it simply an impulsive moment of ink?

The tattoo had to take hours, especially with full color. Nothing about it was impulsive. The urge to offer comfort is so strong, I place my hand on the door.

What am I doing?

Walking into a room with a sleeping woman, uninvited, unsupervised? Hell no. I move my hand down the panel and close the door gently.

In the shower, I can't shut my mind off as easily as I shut her door. Images of her butterfly framed by my ropes, her flying in the air, her curled in a ball, not in her bed but in my restraints as I rail my cock into her welcoming body. I press my hands to the tile wall, rest my forehead between them, searching for control. My cock is not on board with that plan. Hard and aching, it throbs with the need to fuck deep into her and never leave.

This intensity makes no sense. I don't even know her. I don't trust her. I can't get her out of my head.

The soap is in my hand, and I give up the fight. One slow long stroke from tip to root, and I'm weak-kneed and moaning. With each slide of my hand, the rope wraps around her naked body, framing her lush breasts, rendering her helpless to my control, her wrists tied behind her head, making her own wings, as I send her into flight.

Slowly, I increase the pressure on my cock, my rope sliding along her pussy, the knot right against her clit. My climax builds, and I squeeze tight, holding back the release. My fingers wet with her juices, coaxing her to explode. She softens, trusting my ropes, giving all the control to me.

She'd float in my harness, secure in the knowledge I have her as I thrust my starved desperation deep inside her tight, fluttering walls. I pull out, hold my cock, and spin her to a new position. She's my flying creature, caught in my vines, begging me for a release only I can deliver. Faster, she flies. I'm so deep in her, there's no her or me. She ripples against my cock, squeezing me the way my ropes bind her. Warm, wet splashes of her satisfaction coat my skin.

Cum covers my hand. I turn to face the showerhead. The lonely hot mess skulks down the drain. Shame and satisfaction war within. The ache to make my fantasy a reality despite the risk to me. To her.

How can I lasso this butterfly without breaking her wings?

There's no way.

Is there?

God, I haven't felt this strongly about a woman since I left Texas. Why now? Why her?

I haven't been celibate, not completely. The bunnies at the St. Louis club were always willing to let me rig them up. The club asked me to do demos more times than I can count. And in some of those instances, I was so in the moment, I got my dick wet—well, the condom. Brought the bunny to orgasm while I found release. Never in private, and never without witnessed consent.

My grandpa used to say, "Fool me once, shame on you. Fool me twice, shame on me."

I ain't no fool. Except, I'm feeling pretty foolish about SJ. Is it her red hair? Or her Texas twang? That sweetheart ass her jeans hug so expertly? Is it the wide-eyed stare when she watched the couple at the club? Her fascination? Or her innocence?

Innocence. She's no virgin, but she's not a bunny either. She doesn't crave the ropes, to feel the squeeze again. She has no clue what it would feel like to be tied up. But her breath, her pulse, her exquisite concentration on the scene have wrapped me up in a fantasy. To be her first and initiate her into my web of pleasure.

Damn. I'm getting hard again, craving what I shouldn't want. With a slap of my hand, I shut off the water. Dried off, I climb naked into my bead and wait for the strain of a long day of construction to drag me under. When I finally find peace, it's wrecked with dreams of SJ and vine-wrapped butterflies.

EIGHT

SJ

"Alex, wait." That fucker was trying to escape again. It's five in the morning, and he's already headed for the door. I've been trying to catch him since last Friday, getting up earlier and earlier. Mornings suck, but I can't let this drop.

"My ride's waiting." He doesn't even turn to face me.

I smother the urge to rail about him being an asshole. "I need your help to finish the wording for the website and brochures. They aren't going to write themselves, and I don't want to get anything wrong. If you don't have time, I can ask Stone or someone else, but—"

"Tonight." He opens the door.

"What time?" If he makes a promise, he'll keep it. I've seen that much.

"I'll be back for dinner. Stone's grilling."

Thank you, Stone.

Alex finally faces me, one foot out the door. "We can work after we eat."

Almost an invitation. Look at him being all gentlemanly. I smile, but it's more feral than friendly. "Perfect."

The door closes soundlessly between us. I march back upstairs to my bed for a nap, or whatever it's called when you have to get up at the ass crack of dawn to wrangle a jackass into the corral, and a couple more hours of sleep are required before being fully human.

After my second sleep, I spend the day researching rope ties and techniques and how to plot a romance novel until my brain is mush. I've been trying to write details about my characters, and the hero is eerily similar to Alex. How can I write a monster as my hero? But is he? The Alex I know, not the one my uncle has described. Could he have misunderstood Alyss's relationship with Alex? Because when I think back, all I remember is how much Alyss gushed about the guy she was dating. He was perfect—a football player, a gentleman. Maybe I'm the monster for trying to catch him at something so my uncle can get payback for everything he thinks Alex did.

I drop my head in my hands, tears stinging the corners of my eyes. My life is a series of bad decisions and compounding shit. Every time I turn around, someone is taking something from me. Leaving me in a worse position than where I started. If I'd stayed working in the diner, instead of trying to be a model, my uncle wouldn't have had to save me. Now I'm supposed to somehow get dirt on my cousin's ex, catch him in a compromising situation, and I can hardly even catch him in a *conversation*.

I can't see how this will end the way my uncle wants.

A knock at my door startles me out of my doom spiral. Amy's on the other side.

"Hey, I know you're writing, but the guys are grilling. You're welcome to join us. There's plenty."

I glance back at the narrow table I'm using as a desk. The idea of returning to that chair is repulsive. "Sure. That'd be great. Let me clean up, and I'll be down."

Amy gives a tiny hop and flashes a huge smile. "Great."

She's so nice and outgoing. I used to be more friendly. Used to love people. What's she going to think of me when she finds out I was sent here for nefarious reasons? My stomach turns, and I regret agreeing to dinner. But I gave my word, so I find a clean top and freshen up in the bathroom before forcing myself down the stairs. But once I'm on the ground floor, the insecurity of not belonging freezes me in place.

There's a crowd of people like the first night. Stone is at the grill. Amy and Tyler are making trips back and forth to the kitchen. Eliot is back along with Cade, each with a beer. No Alex.

"You going out there or what?" The familiar Texas twang in my ear has me spinning around and practically falling into Alex's arms.

I lurch back.

"Whoa." He grabs my shoulders before I topple over. "Didn't mean to scare you. Figured you would've heard me coming down the stairs."

I swallow, searching for composure and inexplicably

fighting the urge to rub up against him. He's wearing a clean white T-shirt, black denim, and black cowboy boots. His hair is damp on the ends. Freshly showered, he smells like soap and water...and man. That indescribable musky heat. The urge to bury my nose in his neck catches me off guard. I step out of his hold.

He drops his arms. "You okay?"

"Good." I clear the squeak in my voice. "Hungry." That's no lie. I'm starving for this man, and I'm not at all sure what to do about the urge to push up his shirt and run my tongue along his cut abs. Retreat to the patio is my only option, but he's right on my heels. My body is acutely aware of exactly where he is, like a spider with a new victim wiggling in its web. I'm all for wrapping him up tight and taking him and this conversation to the bedroom.

Not gonna happen.

Alex pulls out a chair for me. I almost miss the gesture, it's so unexpected. Who does that anymore? A flutter of uncertainty makes me awkward in my own body.

"Thanks," I say as he scoots the seat forward as I drop into it. He settles easily into the chair at the head of the table, leaving space between us and stretching out his long legs—completely relaxed.

"How's the club coming?" Stone calls from the grill, saving me from making conversation.

Alex stiffens and sits up. "The painters are almost done. Bathrooms are done."

"All of them?" Stone sounds surprised.

"Tile to towel dispensers. Put up the last one before I finished for the day. I would've stayed longer—"

Stone interrupts. "You've been living there."

"Have to. I spend all day managing the subs. Still gotta get my work done."

Stone shoots Alex a look filled with doubt. Does Stone think he's avoiding me too?

"How's the copy coming for the website, SJ?"

I startle. Now *I'm* in Stone's crosshairs. I sit up taller, searching for the right words. I catch myself about to twist my finger in my hair and push it back off my face instead. Sticking with the truth, I answer, "Good. Slow, but good. Alex is helping me with some questions after dinner."

Another laser-guided glare from Stone toward Alex. Before Stone can say a word, Alex pipes up, "I'm on it, boss. We'll have something for Katherine soon."

Ha. *He* got the virtual spanking from Daddy. Now he *has* to help me. I breathe out, releasing the tension in my jaw.

Amy places a bin of silverware in the center of the table and passes plates around before she sits opposite me with a smile. Tyler is right beside her as usual, handing Alex a beer. "Move over. Let me sit next to my wife."

Alex glances at me like he's assessing a threat, but he shifts over one chair to sit next to me. My body lights up in awareness of his proximity. If anything, that's another mark against him. Like my uncle reminded me, I don't pick good men. He shifts his chair away from me.

I open my mouth to tell him I don't bite, but the smell of the steaks makes my stomach grumble.

Alex grins at me with a twinkle of mischief in his eye. I glare, daring him to say something, but he sips his beer as if nothing happened. Why does he have to be so damn attractive? Everything would be so much easier if Alex were a monster on the outside or rude or mean to kittens. Something other than an adorable, sexy, tall cowboy.

"How's Blake?" Amy asks Cade and Eliot.

Cade looks away. Eliot tilts his head in contemplation and finally responds. "Physically, getting better faster than expected."

"It can't be easy for him. For any of you." Amy's focused on Cade, who faces the group after another beat.

"It helped when you came to see him," Cade says. "He needed space from Eliot and me." Cade blinks and tilts his head back to the sky. "I just wish there was more I could do."

It's obvious Cade is tied in knots over the situation.

"He's in the best facility." Tyler's tone is matter of fact.

Cade shrugs and nods.

"Sucks that it's four hours away. I'd see him every day if I could." Alex sounds so sincere.

I glance at him. He's staring into his beer, his shoulders slumped with the weight of friends' burdens.

"But the resort isn't going to build itself."

Stone crosses the patio with a plate of steaming steaks. "We wouldn't be where we are if you hadn't stepped up, Alex, but you can't work twenty-four-seven."

"I'm not. I haven't slept at the site, even though I do lose some time in the commute."

Stone narrows his gaze and makes a low sound of understanding or disbelief. "Pandora is doing a big event this weekend for the holiday. Two days. We're going."

No one responds immediately, too busy filling their plates. I can't do what Stone's demanding. If I go with them to Pandora, I'll be torn between trying to catch Alex doing something bad and convincing him to do bad things to me. My uncle would be pissed. Say I'm wasting an opportunity. But he asked me to get information. I don't have to drown in temptation to do that. I can stay here and work on my book.

After a few minutes of hands and utensils criss-crossing the table, everyone settles in for the feast. I take the first bite of steak and moan. Alex shudders and stiffens, his back ramrod straight. I moan again, on purpose this time. "This is so good."

Stone grins. "Glad you like it."

"I can't remember the last time I had a steak cooked on the grill. Too long."

Alex gives me a curious look as if he's requesting an explanation, but I ignore it. I can't explain how my entire life unraveled. It's been years, and I still haven't fully returned to normal. Maybe after I leave Colorado. Maybe never.

"When's Reed coming out?" Tyler asks.

Who's that? I glance around the table, not sure who Tyler was addressing.

Eliot puts his fork down. "The original contract

finished in December, but the client insisted on a six-month extension to transition to a new security company. We couldn't say no, but I did insist it was the last one. They, like Reed, haven't made any effort to find another bodyguard. But June is it. No more."

"Can he fly out for the weekend?" Stone asks.

Eliot shakes his head. "Holiday and all that. Lots of activities."

"He's been flying back when he can," Cade adds. "Hard to get all the way out to Alabaster when he's only able to stay for a couple days. But in August he'll stay."

"Last time I talked to him, he had all the properties rented and the property manager seems to be working out." Eliot sounds as exhausted as Alex should be.

"Where is Reed living?" I ask as casually as I can.

"St. Louis," Eliot answers.

Amy said they all met at a club in St. Louis. That's where Alex was hiding before my uncle found him out here. I file away that detail. Use it to quiet my uncle the next time he calls.

"Not sure I should take off two days—well, three with drive time." Alex saws a bite of steak away from the slab. "The weather's good this time of year." He stuffs the bite into his mouth, staring at his plate. "Gotta have the apartment ready if Reed's moving out. That cottage Tyler rented won't hold all of you." The last part is directed at Eliot.

"Thought you said the inspector has already been out?" Stone asks, but it's not a question.

"It's gotta be perfect for Blake when they move in.

Still have some paint and finish work. Not to mention the fire door to install between the two units. Fire marshal insisted the door we had wasn't good enough."

"Gabe can take point with the subs if any of them are planning to work over the holiday." The tone Stone uses tells me he doesn't believe anyone will be working the long weekend.

Alex looks at me out of the corner of his eye. I tilt my head in an unasked question, but he turns away. Why do I get the impression he's still avoiding me? This is not the behavior of a predator. He opens doors, carries luggage, and is genuinely concerned about his friends. Hardworking. Responsible. Kind. He's more like a hero in the romance novels I've been reading. Too similar to the character that has been forming in my head for my own book. I'm struggling to resolve that the book boyfriend sitting next to me is the monster of my cousin's past, mostly because the more time I spend around him, the more attractive he becomes as a person.

But I've been fooled before.

NINE

ALEX

"Ready to work?"

SJ is leaning back in her chair like a contented cat. Maybe that explains my urge to pet her, cuddle with her. She glances over, eyelids heavy—exactly how she'd look the next morning in my bed. *Nope.* I scoot my chair back, irritated by my reaction to this woman Stone is sticking me with. Stone has the subtlety of a tank. "Daylight's burning."

My momma raised me right, so I pull out the chair and help SJ up. Her hand barely touches mine, but her long, elegant fingers still shoot heat and possibility up my arm. I release her as soon as she's standing. "Let's get this done. I need some sleep."

"We don't— Okay." SJ thanks everyone for dinner, and Amy brushes off her offer to help clean up.

I follow her inside, nearly running her over when she

stops unexpectedly to ask, "Where should we work? My room or yours?"

An image of working her in my bedroom, her tied, naked, to the frame, flashes through my brain straight to my dick. "Neither." The word explodes out of me in a growl. I clear my throat. "How about we work down here? We can sit at the table or lounge on the couches. Up to you."

She swivels her attention between the two spaces. "The couches. Let me grab my notebook. Be right back."

My eyes are glued to her perfect ass as she bounds up the stairs. I'm grateful when I lose sight of her and I can breathe again. What the fuck is this woman doing to me? I can't be around her at all without getting a damned chub.

The mental list of tasks still remaining at the worksite, along with all the issues I'm having with the subs, works to soften my dick so I can sit comfortably. I drop into the corner of the couch that faces the fireplace. SJ can take the other couch, and we'll still be close enough to talk. At least that's the plan, but she wrecks that, and any composure I gained with my mental checklist, when she drops on the cushion next to me, eyes wide with false innocence.

She knows exactly what she's doing to me.

I know exactly what I'd like to do to her.

I also know what a bad idea it would be.

I shift into the corner, putting a tiny bit more space between us, as if that matters. The soft scent of her, like peaches and vanilla ice cream on a hot summer day, teases me. Only way out of this is through. "Ask away."

"What makes going to a sex club appealing to people, and why will the Yacht Club be better or more unique than the others?"

She doesn't hold her punches. "For one, there's no club like it in the area. Pandora serves their community, and it feels that way, casual, like a community center in any town, but instead of weight benches and a pool, they have spanking benches and St. Andrews crosses."

She stops scribbling. "Won't your club have those things?"

"Of course, but the level of delivery will be different. Less local gym, more fantasy vacation. High-end finishes, polished stained floors. Leather, sound-proofed walls. Instead of folding tables and chairs, booths with privacy curtains, a main stage for demos and guest appearances." I rub my neck. I shouldn't be the one selling this. I'm the construction guy. "The restaurant will be five-star too. The guys interviewed a bunch of chefs. Got a new hotshot looking to earn her first Michelin Star. And then there's the resort itself."

"What about it?" She leans closer, those blue eyes hanging on my next words. So naturally submissive, and she probably isn't even aware.

"Luxury condos and first-class service. It will have all the amenities, of course: a full gym and a huge pool. Two, actually. Half a dozen hot tubs. We're already starting to take reservations, and phase one won't be complete until late September."

"Phase one?"

"Building it in stages. First the restaurant and the dungeon."

"Dungeon? Will you really call it that?"

So innocent. "Yes. Maybe not on the website that faces the public. But there will be a way for those who know to invite people. Everyone will be vetted."

"Everyone?"

Why does that sound like an accusation? "Absolutely."

"How did you get into tying people up?"

Where the heck did that question come from? It has nothing to do with the website or marketing. I could refuse to answer. I rub the back of my neck. She's probably just curious. Can't just boop her on the nose and tell her no like a naughty kitten. "Kind of a long story."

"Not going anywhere."

"When I was a kid, I was kind of small."

Her gaze glides up and down my body. "Hard to believe."

"It's true. My older sister tried to help. Convinced me to punch the bully who was making my life hell." I fucking hated that dude. George Conrad. The memory of his smug face and evil glee when he targeted the smaller kids hasn't faded.

"Did you hit him?"

"Yeah. I balled up my fist and gave my best shot right into his gut."

"And?" She leans closer, her hand on my thigh.

And let's go upstairs. "He laughed and pushed me

down in the lunch line. Thought he was going to kick me, but the lunch lady stepped in.”

“Did he get in trouble?” Her frown mimics the one my sister had so long ago, disgusted with a possible injustice.

“Three-day suspension. He promised to kill me as soon as he got back. I told my daddy I was done with school and focusing on ranching from that day on.”

She laughs, and her whole face lights up. “I can see you, ‘little’ Alex, announcing your plans. Stomping your booted foot. How’d that work out?”

“Not as well as I’d planned.” I grin at the remembrance of the utter shock on my daddy’s face. “Luckily, my sister stepped in. She had a flyer from school about a martial arts place running classes on Wednesdays after school, and they even had a bus to pick us up.” I shrug because one thing led to another. It’s obvious.

“So you attended karate class, and that led to ropes?” Her forehead wrinkles. So dang cute.

“Jiujitsu. It was the coolest thing I’d ever done. Different from everything that came before. As far from Texas and ranching as a boy could get. I was hooked—had to know everything about it. I checked books out of the library. That led to Hojojutsu as I got older. Eventually, I convinced the sensei to help me with some of the ties. I was well familiar with working with ropes on the ranch. Hell, I even did some rodeo events.”

Her face softens and she stares at me for a quiet moment, as if she can see me as a kid.

“But roping on the ranch is nothing like Shibari.”

"What about your bully?"

"He backed off. Turns out, the older kids in the jiujitsu class didn't put up with anyone picking on the younger ones. I think they made it clear to George that if he hit me again, they would spend an afternoon teaching him what it felt like to get picked on my someone bigger."

"So this bully George is to blame for you hanging out in dungeons and tying up woman?" Her tone is teasing, but there's something deeper in the question.

I give her the most irreverent answer I can to hopefully stop her digging into me and my past. "I should probably write him a thank-you note or something."

"Rodeos and jiujitsu explains your fascination with rope. But how does that translate into BDSM? I'm guessing your small town didn't have a dungeon."

Doesn't sound like a guess. But I didn't mention how big the town was. "Wasn't too small for an internet connection. You'd be amazed what videos are to be found if you dig deep enough."

She drops her head and her cheeks turn red.

"Or maybe you wouldn't be. Done some surfing?"

"A bit. But back to the Yacht Club." She scoots away, adjusting her notebook. "If you could only tell people one thing about it, what would you say?"

"It's a bucket list experience."

"What do you mean?" she asks, scribbling more notes.

"There are a lot of dungeons out there. Some people even host events in their home, converted basements and all that."

She nods as if she's trying to figure out who she knows with a basement.

"But the Yacht Club will be complete indulgence. Best food, best relaxation, best dungeon. Few will be able to afford a membership, but many will be able to splurge on a once-in-a-lifetime visit."

"How will you keep people from being outed? I imagine some of the extremely wealthy are also famous."

"Without pictures, you can't prove it ever happened. They might say something to their friends who are in the community, but even if they say something more publicly, who'll believe them? Pics or it never happened, right?"

"Right." She rolls her lower lip between her teeth, her gaze drops to her notebook, and she goes silent.

Did I say something rude? "Eliot and his crew are experts in security. They won't let anything happen. You wouldn't believe the wiring they had me build into the place. Pretty sure I could run a data center in the basement if the dungeon fails."

She barely reacts, only a hint of a nod.

"Did you have any more questions?" Please talk to me again. I'm a total bastard, and I don't even know what I've done.

SJ clutches her notebook to her chest and stands. "No. I'm good. Thanks."

I stand too, but she backs away. This is like a scene gone wrong, but I can't release my ropes and cuddle her to make it better.

She's nearly at the stairs when I call out, "Bring your

questions this weekend. Everyone will be in the car, and you can get more than my stupid country-ass opinion."

She pauses mid-step, one foot on the stair, hand on the rail. Her gaze pins me in place. "You're far from stupid, Alex. And I love the country."

Her words pierce through a protective layer around my heart I wasn't aware was there until she busted it wide open. I rush around the sofa, but by the time I clear the open living room and get to the stairs, I only catch the briefest glimpse of her as she darts down the hallway. I swear I hear her sob. What the fuck did I do?

The stairs slow me down because I don't want to break my neck on the Victorian-era treads. Not designed for my big ole feet. One of which I must have shoved in my mouth back there. She's almost to her room. "SJ?"

My call doesn't slow her. She's in the room, door closed, lock snicking into place. I grip the frame and lean my forehead against the door. "I'm sorry," I say in a low whisper.

I have no clue what I did, but I hurt her, and I don't know how to fix it.

The bigger issue is that I want to.

TEN

SJ

The question-and-answer session with Alex last night wasn't a total waste, despite my losing my shit when he mentioned pictures. Up until that moment, the sore spot had been hidden for years. But his gentle reference tore me open, and grief ripped through me. The loss of my innocence. The humiliating exposure. My uncle seeing me like that. The morally gray situation I find myself in. I like Alex. He's a genuinely nice person, and I'm supposed to help ruin his life?

He's already gone when I finally drag myself to breakfast. Amy, so super sweet, only adds to my guilt with her offers of coffee and fresh-cooked eggs. I can't be here strictly as an author now, so I choose to hide in my room and work on writing as if that will erase the fact I'm supposed to hurt Alex. Thankfully, the wording for the website comes together easily.

Sail into your dream vacation.

Cruise into elegance.

Your fantasy is dead ahead.

You can't fathom how good life can be until you stay at the Yacht Club.

I could keep writing these phrases for days, playing with the words, but I'm distracted by the characters of my book.

Shelly sailed into the dungeon, searching for the Dom who had captured her in his web. She wasn't a submissive, swore she wouldn't be caught in his net again, but his wry smile and blue-eyed gaze destroyed her resistance. The club called to her like a siren seduced unwary sailors. The rocks loomed, but she couldn't protect herself.

There. Onstage. Rope in his hand, he wound it around and around the black-haired beauty, each tightly controlled wrap squeezing the air from Shelly's chest, slicing into her heart.

The muscles of his bare back rippled. The dark leather pants showcased the line of his ass, the lean tension in his thighs. She moved closer as he caressed the naked woman's nipple. The touch shot through Shelly's body like a harpoon, as if she were the one in his embrace. Tears pricked her eyes.

Yes, she'd stayed away. Told him she would never return. But he had to know she was a liar. Had to know she couldn't live without him. He glanced up. Caught her eye and dropped his line. Her heartbeat stuttered as he fumbled. For a moment, they were both frozen, connected but unable to bridge the distance that gaped between their bodies. He turned, whispered in the ear of his bunny.

Shelly couldn't watch any more. She shouldn't have returned to his lair. She spun and raced up the stairs, away from the dungeon and what was left of her ability to love.

I think it's good. Maybe a bit overwritten, but the dark moment is supposed to be dark. There are too many nautical references; I've been distracted by the copy for the club. Or not distracted but infused. If I want this book to be something worth publishing, I should focus on the bondage aspect, not sirens and sailors. Although, that'd be a great name for the bar at the club. I write it down in my notebook before I shift my attention back to my laptop and the Shibari sites I've bookmarked.

I stumble onto rope videos on a free porn site. Most of them are too harsh for me, and I quickly click away. But this one guy... He's not attractive to me, too skinny. But the more I watch, the deeper I'm pulled. There are dozens of films. Each with a different woman, all shapes and sizes. He adores them. The ropes are like paintbrushes in the hands of an artist; he wraps their bodies up safely so they can relax completely and he can pleasure them. This bondage lights me up.

He slides his cock slowly into one of his partners, its length disappearing into the V of her bound thighs. Her eyes soften, lids lower, and her breath catches as he fills her completely. My body craves that feeling. I sneak my fingers inside my pants, underneath the elastic of the panties.

I'm wet.

My fingers slip along my lips easily, teasing my clit.

He moves faster, his narrow hips bucking into the

softness of her. He grasps coils of his rope around her body, securing her in place so that he can fuck her to orgasm. The image blurs, and it's Alex's arms holding the ropes, Alex riding the woman I imagine is me.

I follow his pace, teasing my clit, fucking my pussy.

Her mouth opens in a silent scream and her back arches. He slides his hand to the front of her pussy and works her clit like I'm working mine. The other hand still holds her close, her position exactly what he designed. His pace quickens, jutting into her, his glistening length making teasing appearances. I can almost imagine my fingers are his cock. One last thrust and his body goes rigid, arcing deep into his partner. I release with him, shaking and coming. Clenching my jaw to keep from calling out his name.

As my panting slows and I can finally breathe again, I close the browser window into the strangers' intimacy. I glance at the door. Did I make noise? Did Alex hear me? Did I lock the door? Alex could be right outside, listening to me get myself off. He could open the door and catch me watching porn and fingering myself. He could tie me up, wrap me in his ropes, and fuck me senseless.

It's a fantasy, and it needs to stay that way. Remain research for the website—for my book. But to write the story, I have to understand what it means to be bound willingly on every level: physically, emotionally, sexually. Several videos give instructions on how to self-tie, and I have them bookmarked.

I need rope.

Now.

I wash my hands and straighten my clothes, pulling my wild hair into a ponytail. My skin has a healthy glow from the pleasure I gave myself. I want more.

Minutes later, I'm pulling my rental car into a parking spot in front of a block of storefronts. They remind me of a postcard from the 1950s, all picture glass windows framed in brick with store names in gold or red or blue vinyl stickers. The hardware store I found online is in the middle of the cluster, and the sign on the door is turned to *Open*. A bell that's tied to the handle inside rings as I push the door open. An elderly man behind a green Formica counter with a cash register on top calls out a greeting, despite being busy ringing up items for a man in overalls.

I wave and duck into the shelves, not ready to ask for help finding what I need. The place is crowded with all the things a homeowner might need—hammers, screwdrivers, and other hand tools. Racks of nails and screws in more sizes than anyone could possibly need. Showerheads and faucets. Sprinklers and spools of tubing. There's a little display in the back with paint swatches. Finally, I find a garden section with twine for tying up vegetables. Not useful for my purpose. I keep searching.

"Can I help you find anything?"

I jump, and a squeal squeaks out.

"I'm so sorry, miss. Didn't mean to surprise you." He takes a step back—same guy who was running the register. Not a threat. Not even scary. "You seem like you're looking for something specific. Figured I could help you."

"I need some rope?" I can't even make it a statement.

"Cotton, nylon, jute?"

"Cotton." Sounds like softest option. And I flash back to my grandmother hanging clothes on the line outside. "And clothespins."

His smile is once again at ease. I've given him something he can work with, and I relax because I don't have to explain myself. "Sundried laundry smells so fresh."

He wanders back down the aisle, and I follow him to the housewares section. Wouldn't have guessed. But the clothesline, coiled in a figure eight inside a plastic bag, is exactly what I pictured. Not quite what they use in the videos, but it should work. The man adds a pack of clothespins, and I almost blow it and tell him I don't need those. But they're cheap, so I nod and let him ring me up.

I can't drive back to the inn fast enough. It's nearly dinnertime, but luckily no one expects me to join them for the meal. I could stop and grab takeout, but I'll get something later if I'm hungry. The only thing that matters right now is getting the rope on my skin.

Back at the inn, I dart up the stairs, relieved not to have to explain myself to anyone. Not sure how I would explain the outdoor laundry equipment with any kind of believability. With the door locked, I strip down to my underwear, retrieve the rope, and toss the bag on the bed. The plastic wrapper fights me, but I finally rip it open and unwind the length. It dangles from one hand as I navigate to my instruction videos with the other. With a tap on the pad on my laptop, the first video starts.

I sit on the ground and try the first tie around my ankle. The instructions are clear. Keep the line straight like a stick. Stay in control, using the rope as an extension of my hands. The videos are fast, and I can't tie the knots and complete the wraps and pause the playback. It's frustrating, and there's none of the erotic appeal. With a huff, I stop the instruction and release my thigh and ankle. There are a bunch of other videos, so I watch one on basic knots. She's talking about knots I learned to tie as a kid. Another video teaches quick release knots. I have no idea which one I should try first. The basics seem like an easier place to start. Following along, I almost manage to tie my ankles together, but the rope doesn't lie the way the instructor showed. The search for other simple ties I can complete on myself leads to love handles and breast harnesses. Too difficult. I try a single column tie on my wrist. It kind of works once I get my thumb in the loop they call the bite. The terminology confuses me, but I'm trying to tighten the wrap to make it look like the image.

A knock at the door jolts me. I click stop on the video and pull the rope, barely getting it hidden in a drawer when a second, firmer knock echoes through my room. "Coming."

"SJ? Are you okay?"

The calming breath I take as I crack open the door does nothing to slow my heartbeat. Neither does the man propped against the doorframe.

I hide my mostly naked body behind the door and shoot my leg out to the frame, creating a barrier to him entering. The bag of clothespins on the bed grows ten times in size, demanding an explanation I can't give. Better to keep him out. "Did you need something?"

He turns his attention from my face to my wrist, and the corners of his mouth turn up. The devil dances in his eyes. "What have you been up to, little rabbit?"

My mouth moves, but not even a squeak comes out.

Alex wraps his hand around my wrist and steps forward into the opening, into my body—almost a hug.

Heat flashes through me, starting right between my legs and cresting like a wave up my neck to my cheeks. I must be cherry red with a blush this hot. He takes two more steps forward, and I grip his shoulder to keep from falling backward; instead, it's as if I'm falling into him, losing all sense of reality. He lowers my arm between us and opens his fingers. "Care to explain these marks?"

A deep shiver rattles my bones. "Promise not to judge?"

ALEX

She thinks I'd shame her? Over *this*? In my wildest dreams, I didn't see her as a rope bunny. And she's not. Not yet.

"Little rabbit. I'm not judging, but I won't let you hurt yourself." She allows me to guide her toward the bed, where a laptop is frozen on a Shibari training video from a reputable site. But based on the marks on her skin, the instructions didn't capture the subtle details that make rope bondage pleasurable instead of damaging. "Show me the rope you were using."

She tugs her arm, but I can't release her. I gaze into

her eyes. There's a mix of fear and shame but, most importantly, desire. I step closer, our bodies nearly touching, holding her hand down by my side. When she doesn't move, I shift my hold on her to a caress along the length of her slender arm, along her shoulder, up into her hair. Threading my fingers through her red mane, I tug her head back with enough bite to get her attention. Her mouth goes slack, and her attention is fully on me. Fuck. She's gorgeous. Perfect. "Get the rope."

The tiny nod she manages works like a key to unlocking my grip on her. She moves to the dresser and bends over, her heart-shaped ass in the perfect position to receive my cock. I palm my hardened length down, trying to regain some control over myself. SJ spins, the rope behind her back but dangling, I catch a glimpse of clothesline and bite back a bark of laughter. *We all start somewhere.*

And she has well and truly started.

She takes the two steps, returning to me, her head low, rope still clutched behind her.

"Show me."

Her throat undulates with a thick swallow. I lift my hand, repeating my demand wordlessly. She tilts her head, looking for reassurance. She must find what she needs because the rope lands in my hand. I carefully inspect it and consider my words, letting silence do my work. When she fidgets, shifting her weight from one foot to the other, I say, "It's not ideal. And your placement is dangerous."

She nods. "I had trouble hooking the bite to tighten it."

"Stay. Right. Here." I drop the rope on the bed and leave her to get one of my ropes. I've procrastinated on bundling them in preparation for our trip. I wrap one of the lengths in a long coil, more cowboy than rigger, but it works. She's exactly where I left her. "Good little rabbit." I hold out the coil between us. "This is quality Shibari rope. You are not wet clothes in need of a little sunshine. You are a priceless gift, and if you want me to, I'll show you—"

She lifts her arms to me, forearms pressed together, wrists exposed. Vulnerable. Submissive. Her trusting gaze stabs into me, locking me in place. So soft. So sweet. "Please."

I turn her forearms so her hands can clasp, but I press them flat into a prayer position and begin. My body leads from muscle memory, allowing me to enjoy every sigh, every shiver. Every shift in balance as she tenses and relaxes. It's our dance. And it's beautiful. I spin her into my arms, wrapping her with my body so I can hold her as I ladder the rope up her arms, creating beautiful knots down the center. I lose track of time as she softens in my hold. The final end tucked inside, it's a perfect binding.

She turns her head, lips so close to mine. I could bend and take what she's offering. Her eyes are glazed with the bliss of submission, and only her arms are bound. The pleasure she could find if I wrapped her entire body. Pleasure I could give her. I could easily sweep her up in my arms right now, lay her on the bed, and work those jeans off her sweet ass. Plunge inside. My cock twitches.

Fuck.

Too much.

The door is open. For a reason. So I don't spiral out of control, because she could make me forget my rules. Make me forget why I have rules. Make me forget that I can't have this kind of intimacy.

She's exactly what I dreamed of finding in a sub. And I can't have her. Can't trust anyone so intimately again. There are reasons I only play in a club and only so take my games so far.

I tug the quick release I formed when I placed the series of knots. They cascade free, leaving the rope limp and without purpose. I coil it up quickly, avoiding her vulnerable questioning gaze. The answers I have wouldn't satisfy her or explain anything. "Keep this."

She accepts the coil with shaking hands.

An apology forms in my throat, but I can't say it. I squeeze her grip around the rope once, briefly, and fly from her room to the safety of my own.

Maybe it could work. If I didn't have the past I have. SJ reminds me how sweet a connection like ours can be. I found submission like this once before. Risked and lost everything for it. Could I take that risk again?

ELEVEN

SJ

Amy fills my cup of coffee while I slather one of her delicious lavender scones with lemon curd. I've got to do a workout today—a long one. Get my head on straight, because Alex literally has me tied in knots. An extended yoga session will do the trick to clear the confusion and get rid of some the pastry calories I've been consuming.

"Are you packed?"

"What?"

"For the weekend in Colorado Springs. Pandora? I assumed you were going. For research."

If I do, there's no way I won't be bound in Alex's ropes and naked in his bed. It was a close thing last time. There's no way I could resist after I've gotten to know him better, after I've found the taste for being tied up. The way he bound my arms, so tenderly, so tight, with perfect precision and symmetry. The effect was nearly overwhelming, and the urge to drop to my knees—I choke on a crumb of scone. Tyler pats my back until I can take a breath. A sip of coffee helps to clear the sensation of airless panic. I wipe the tears from my eyes. "I have to work this weekend. My agent is not happy with my progress. He's given me an extension, if I can stay a little longer?"

"Of course. I don't have anyone else booked for the room."

Amy said the room was open when I checked in, but it's nice to have the confirmation. I'll have to ask my uncle for permission to stay as well, but that can wait. "I'd love to visit Pandora again, maybe before I leave?"

"Sure. And don't worry about this weekend. Tyler and I can stay here." Amy plasters a fake smile on her face. Tyler flashes a frown at me but nods reassuringly at Amy.

Stone has an unreadable expression, and Eliot and Cade are ignoring everything, filling their plates.

"I'll stay." Alex's voice is behind me, and I jump in my seat, hopefully not enough to notice. But I'm sitting next to Tyler, and he's looking at me like I'm a clue on a murder board. "I'll take point on the inn so you and Tyler can go. Besides, I found a fireproof door in stock in Denver. I've got it on hold, but that crew isn't available again for a couple weeks and they'll only hold it for forty-eight hours. Gabe and I are getting it tomorrow. I'll probably finish up the painting too."

Not good. He's who I'm trying to avoid. I shoot a plaintive look to Amy, but her focus is on Stone. His expression hasn't altered—blank slate.

Amy's gaze flits from Tyler, to the buffet, to Alex, and she swipes a hair that escaped from her ponytail. "I have plenty of food, eggs and bacon. And there are bagels in the freezer. They'll need to be thawed and toasted. Cream cheese is in the same bin as the butter."

Alex grips her in a one-armed side hug. "I got this. Managed to feed myself for years before coming out here. And I promise not to let SJ starve either."

"She skips meals," Amy says.

Are they seriously talking about me in front of me?

Alex nods. "I know." How could he know? He's never here. And why would he bother to notice? "I promise to make sure she's taken care of and has plenty of writing time. I'll even make her a sack lunch when I make mine." His tone is teasing, and he's slanting one of his sweet, Southern-charm grins at me. And *dang it*, it works.

Why does he have to be so nice? So adorable? He's supposed to be a monster. It would be so much easier if he acted like what he was. Or maybe not. Maybe I can't condemn someone for their past when I know how situations can spiral out of control in seconds.

After breakfast, I hide in my room and write in between long sessions of staring at my keyboard. Not sure I can do this—get an entire novel written. It'll probably be horrible. But I have to try. The book was the reason I came out here. Maybe not the reason my uncle sent me, but I didn't know that when I hopped on the plane. At least by writing the book, I'm not a complete liar, only mostly.

There's a rush after lunch, suitcases dragging from

the rooms and down the stairs. Conversations in the hall about where they're staying and if Cade and Eliot need a hotel room. It hits me that these people are a family. They care for each other in all the ways a family should. All the ways my family used to. Before my dad and mom divorced. Before Alyss moved away from Texas with her mom. Before I made the worst decision of my life.

Was my family ever really normal, or was it the make-believe innocence of my childhood? Do Cade and Eliot and Amy and Tyler realize what they are to each other? Does Stone? What will happen to this family when I take Alex from them? Can I do that? Break them apart for a man who claims to be my family but who isn't interested in protecting me at all?

My gut churns, and the little bit of food I ate at Amy's insistence threatens to reappear. The book can wait. I have to lie down right now.

Heavy footsteps coming up the stairs rouse me from the half-dreaming state I've been lazing about in. I must have slept for hours because the summer sun is brilliant but low in the sky. Any minute, sunset will paint the sky in oranges and reds before the stars blink into being. I should get up and at least open the sheers. Appreciate this beautiful space before I ruin it and my chances for coming back someday.

I drag myself out of bed. Everyone left hours ago, so it must be Alex I heard. I wash my face and freshen my makeup for dinner. The hallway of the inn feels colder, wider, and so empty. I glance to my left, toward Alex's room. I should wait for him downstairs. But when I step out, I turn toward his room. With slow, hesitant steps, I close the distance.

His door gapes the tiniest bit, like he shoved it closed but it didn't latch. A deep grunt filters into the hallway and hits my neck as if it was my throat making the sound, shooting a sensation of longing and seduction right into my brain. What is he doing? I can't see inside unless I were to lean on the door or maybe knock. But I don't want to disturb him. Another grunt or moan. Is there a word for both? Not a great time to search the thesaurus.

"Fuck. SJ."

That does it. I place my palm on the door and push.

Oh. My. Fucking. Damn.

Alex is fully stretched out on the bed, naked, muscles in his arms rippling as he strokes the most gorgeous cock I've ever seen with one hand and grasps the headboard with the other. That dim encounter in the hotel between the rooms while he hid himself behind his hands didn't prepare me for hard, masturbating Alex. The way the muscles in the V of his pelvis tense and relax as he fucks his hand. The way his entire body arches up with need. He's fucking glorious.

"SJ," he grunts as his cum splashes over his hand on to his laddered abs.

I must make a noise, because he bolts up, grabbing the towel next to him and covering himself. So disappointing.

"Tie me." I'm not sure why that's what I say, but it's the truest thing in this moment. I want him to tie me to the bed and fuck me until I come as hard as he did.

"What? What are you doing?" Alex drops his head. "I'm sorry. I shouldn't have been doing that. Give me a minute, and I'll clean up. We can have dinner and—"

"I want you to tie me up."

He jerks his attention to me, his eyes wide. "No way."

I slip off my shirt and drop it to the ground. "Please?"

He shakes his head, his gaze locked on my chest.

"There's nothing stopping us." I unclasp my bra and cup myself with my hands.

Alex blinks and then finally looks at me. I peel away the fabric and let the straps slide down my shoulders. He grips the towel and presses down on his cock. Nice recovery. I prop a breast in each hand, lifting them, and pinch each nipple between my thumb and forefinger until I gasp and arch into the pain that shoots into my pussy. "You made me so wet."

"What are you doing?"

I drop my hands and pop the button on my shorts. "Guess."

"You shouldn't."

The zipper rasps as I pull the tab. A moment later, the fabric is pooled at my bare feet. I step out. Closer to him.

"We can't."

I slip my fingers inside my panties and pull the wetness onto my clit, making slow, easy circles as I lock my gaze on him. Faster. My fingers move to match my need.

"Stop."

His command freezes me.

"Show me."

Oh fuck yes. I free my hand and stuff my juicy fingers in my mouth. Alex groans. Then his lips are on mine. I barely saw him move. His kiss is so hot, my legs start to melt. But too quickly, it's over. He drops to his knees at my feet. My panties are in his hands, down my legs.

"Step out."

I grip his shoulder for balance and follow his instruction with pleasure. He's so damn tall, his eyes are practically right at boob level. But he's not interested in boobs. He lifts my leg and plants it on his shoulder, spreading me open. Before I can figure out what's happening, I'm cradled in his arms, one arm along my spine, the other holding my ass. I'm not going anywhere. He's locked me down without ropes. "I have to taste you."

It sounds like a request.

I nod.

"Words."

"Yes, Alex. Taste me." Eat me. Make me come on your tongue. I squirm in his hold, not quite believing I said any part of that out loud.

He places a scorching kiss at the apex of my opening, teases my clit with the tip of his tongue and hums his delight.

I'm done for. Putty in his hands. Completely at his mercy.

Slow and certain. Tracking each twitch, every response I give him. He builds my climax and retreats before I can go over. Again. Each rasp of his tongue, each twist of his mouth, each nuzzle of my pussy done with such deliberate intensity, I beg. "Please Alex, please let me come."

He gazes up at me, the lust that wraps me in a tight cocoon radiating from him. I'm an extension of his arms—his plaything. His arms tighten around me, and he returns to his work like a man possessed.

"Please." I chant the word on repeat, lost in the pleasure he's constructing like a cage around me, building the walls, sealing the doors. I'm trapped completely in his care, nothing to do but feel and beg. He sucks so hard on my clit, I feel the tug rip my heart from its anchor in my chest, and I scream with the release of the pressure. He laps at me as my pussy floods his face.

Suddenly I'm flying. In his arms. He's standing, moving me to the bed, following me down. My other leg's over his shoulder, and he buries his face between my legs again.

"I can't."

He presses two fingers deep inside me and twists. "You will."

"Oh damn." He's right, I will come again for him. As many times as he demands.

He eats me to orgasm twice more before I beg him to stop. His cock is hard when he stands by the side of the bed. He didn't fuck me. I slide my hand through the mess he made and use my juices to stroke his length. He puts his knee on the bed, covers my hand with his, increasing the pressure, showing me what he likes. He leans forward and rubs the tip across my lips. My body stiffens, and I turn my head.

I can't.

I try to stroke him again, but he holds me in place as he places distance between us. "Talk to me." Alex's voice is soft but still in command. He hasn't released my hand, I'm still holding his hot length, but everything has stopped. "We clearly hit a limit. So I need you to talk to me right now."

I blink at the wall and swallow down my disappointment in myself. Why can't I get over this? Why do I feel shame about what someone else did to me? Why does it still matter? "I don't give blowjobs. I should have said something before I let you eat me out, but—"

"Stop." He grips my chin, turns my head, and waits until I meet his gaze. "I ate your delicious peach of a pussy because I wanted to. Has nothing to do with you sucking my dick."

"All men want blowjobs." Or pictures of them.

"Doubt it. I'm sure there are some who don't like it, for whatever reason. Who cares why. Don't matter. If *you* don't want to do something, that's enough of a reason. Just tell me. Talk to me." He caresses my face so tenderly.

He's not a monster. No matter what my uncle thinks, he's wrong. Alex is a good man. I slide my hand up his cock. "Don't let this be over. I want to make you feel good. I want to be with you, Alex."

"Wait." He takes a step back.

Fuck, I've lost him. If only I could get over my resistance to this one act.

He grabs a bottle from the nightstand. "We need a little help." He holds my hand palm up and squirts out some of the lube, cold at first but quickly warming against my skin. With a nudge, he makes room on the bed to straddle me on his knees, his cock in full glory. Apparently my lack of oral desire didn't dampen *his* ardor a bit. I grip him as hard as he showed me and work him up and down, learning every vein and bump, savoring the way his skin shifts over the steely core. His hips move to my rhythm. He's over me, topping me, but somehow giving me control. A smile forms on my lips, and I speed up, taking ownership of his pleasure the way he owned mine. I cup his heavy balls, playing a little, and get a moan from him. Yeah, that's it. I swirl my hand over his crown with each stroke, adding pressure as if he was riding me, his length inside me. His cock weeps with pleasure, adding to the lube. I speed up my motions, adding heat, following the silent demands of his body.

"Fuck. Fuck. SJ. I'm gonna come so hard. Do it, baby. Make me come all over those glorious tits."

"Yes." I draw his length down, pointing the tip toward my chest, working his length. He grips my hand again, takes control, and his body freezes in a roar as the first release arcs across my skin. Each shuddering shot paints me with his hot pleasure. The satisfaction of bringing this man to ecstasy makes me glow. He frees himself from my grip, and I gaze into his eyes as I rub his cum into my skin, over my nipples, squeezing my flesh to burnish him into my body. I don't have to swallow him to infuse him into me.

TWELVE

ALEX

I bite my lip and tilt my head back. SJ is too fucking sexy, rubbing my cum into her skin like it's liquid gold. There is nothing I crave more than to work my cock deep into her sweet pussy, but I'm looking at a dangerous ride. No one here to have my back if everything goes sideways. No alibi to confirm she gave consent.

"Alex, I need you." SJ blinks her beautiful baby blues at me.

No way I can walk away.

A stray lock of hair is hiding part of her face. I swipe it back so she can see me clearly. "What do you want exactly? Every single detail."

She reaches for me, and I grip her wrists in one hand, pressing them over her head.

"No touching. Not until we agree on what comes next."

Her tongue swipes across her lip, and my dick wakes up. "You. Fucking me. That's what I want."

"My dick inside that sweet pussy?"

"Yes." Her reply is breathy, and she squirms in my hold.

Not getting off that easy, little rabbit.

"What position? Missionary, doggy, side by side?"

"Any position you want as long as you make me come around your cock. And I want to feel you explode inside me."

"Rough, gentle?"

"Gentle and hard. Fast if we need it. Slow if you want it. Whatever you want."

"No, baby. It's whatever you want. Any other limits besides no oral?" She's lust crazed, but this is serious. I haven't been alone with a woman, since...since forever.

"Don't come on my face."

I nod. Not my kink. "Anal?"

She rolls her bottom lip between her teeth and looks away.

"That's a no." I press a kiss to her lips to seal the deal, my chest against her sweet tits. This woman is like lemonade on a hot day. I crave her. She wiggles under me. The head of my cock grazes her wet heat. The urge to press inside is nearly irresistible. "Hold on."

Condom. Do I have any? I release her arms and shift off my bed. Not in the nightstand or the bathroom. I check my gear bag. If I had any, they'd be there, but I got nothing. "I'll be right back. Don't move."

"Or you could tie me up."

"Naughty rabbit. I could withhold that fuck you want so bad."

Her mouth forms an O before shifting to a pout.

I point at her. "Don't move."

She nods, and I head for the door. Cade or Eliot are sure to have some. I'll replace whatever I take. It's unnerving to walk naked through the inn. Like I'm at home. This is as close to a home as I've had. Living with family again instead of a shitty apartment in a crazy city. Colorado fits me almost as well as Texas. Would SJ ever consider staying?

Damn, I'm getting ahead of myself.

Thankfully, Cade's room is unlocked and there's an open box in his bathroom. I shove my hand in to take a few then let them go and take the whole box. I'm not hunting for a condom again, and once I get my cock inside SJ, I'm not sure I'll be able to stop. It's risky to fuck her, but as long as I leave all the kink out of it—no ropes, no pushing limits, nothing but pure vanilla—I can convince myself there's minimal risk.

She's almost exactly as I left her on the bed. Her arms over her head, hands clasped, her long legs stretched out and parted as if they were tied to the footboard. Frozen in the doorway, I mentally file an image of her. This is never leaving my spank bank. The only way it could be better would be if my ropes were actually wrapped around her.

One step into the room, and the magnitude of what I'm doing hits me like a kicking bull. SJ is beautiful, impossible to resist, but she's leaving. Maybe that's why I'm breaking my rules. She's the most intriguing woman

I've known, ever. Probably because I've had some time to get to know her. When I'm with partners in the club, it's an interaction. A transaction. Terms are agreed on, and we do it then go our separate ways. SJ's not staying either. Unlike my connections in the club, the fact that she'll be gone soon doesn't bring me a sense of ease.

"Everything okay? Box empty?" SJ still hasn't moved, but her eyes are inspecting me.

"Everything's perfect." Mostly, except my head. I tilt the box forward. "All set."

She wiggles her hips as if she's bound to the bed. My cock hears the call of her sweet pussy, and any doubts I had disappear as the blood rushes away from my over-thinking brain. I take my time crossing the short distance to the bed, setting the condoms on the night table and plucking one free. "You ready to ride, little rabbit?"

"Hell, yes."

I tweak her nipple. "Good."

She squeaks and squirms but doesn't shift position, preserving the illusion I've bound her. The foil tears easily, and I roll on the protection. Safety first. Except if I was being safe, I wouldn't be doing this at all. She's somehow broken the barrier I built ten years ago.

I climb onto the bed between her legs and drag my finger between her wet lips. Yeah, she's ready. Am I? My dick twitches like I better be ready because this is happening. A craving for her consumes me. Demands the feel of her wrapped around me. Tugging me deeper. Pulling me in.

No argument left, I lift her hips and notch the head

of my cock at her entrance before pressing slowly forward, savoring each sweet squeeze of her embrace as I shift inside her. More. The word pounds like a drum through my brain. More SJ, more of me inside her, more connection.

Once I'm seated fully in her sweet heat, SJ is panting, her soft gaze on me. I release her hips to rest on my thighs, bend forward, and lift her body into my embrace. I've pinned us in place, but she's so flexible. She adjusts her feet on the mattress and lifts her hips, riding me. So strong. I clutch her close, aiding her movement as I can, letting her take what she wants from me. No one has ever taken control during sex. But this is perfect. Exactly as it should be our first time. I give myself to her, promise her everything with a kiss and hope she understands.

Hope she doesn't break my heart.

Her speed intensifies. Her pussy squeezes me, bringing all my attention to now. The way her fingers dig into my shoulders. The softness of her skin in my arms. It all comes together in an overwhelming stream of energy that moves down my spine to build at the base, coiling, heating. "Come for me, baby."

I press my hand between us and find her clit. If she doesn't come soon, I'll embarrass myself. Not that I wouldn't make it up to her, but I'm not a selfish lover, and I don't want our first time to leave her disappointed. There it is. Her tiny squeaks speed up. She's bouncing on my dick, her tits following the moment, capturing my attention. Fuck me. This woman is a fantasy wrapped in a wet dream. Electric spikes spark from my spine down my legs, up to my chest. My balls tighten. I can't— "Now, baby."

She drops down one last time and stops moving, her back arched into my one-arm embrace. I pinch her clit with a gentle squeeze, and she squeals. Her pussy grips me and sucks me deeper, a rhythmic rolling that makes me lose control. I release into her with a roar. The condom keeps me from painting her insides, but my dick does its best to mark her as mine.

SJ drops her head to my shoulder, panting and boneless. I free my hand and hold her. More than eating her out, more than fucking her senseless, this moment, with her completely at ease in my arms, our skin sweaty and hot but sated and soft, burrows into my heart. I clutch her a little bit tighter to hold myself together. I'm lost in her and a little bit scared that once again I'll lose everything. I don't know if I could survive this time.

THIRTEEN

ALEX

The box of condoms is just out of reach. I roll forward, pressing SJ into the mattress, and free another packet. Not sure how many we've used, but I'm glad I grabbed the box. At some point today, I have to get out of this bed, but not yet. Not until my sweet rabbit comes for me again. She's soft and yielding in my arms, still recovering from me eating her out before she was fully awake. I can't get enough of her, but it feels like she's holding back. Maybe because she's leaving soon? Doesn't matter. She's here now.

"Ready, baby?" One more time, I'll bury myself inside her and avoid reality for a few minutes more.

She wraps her legs around my hips and clutches my shoulders. Her eyes are still filled with the clouds of sleep. She's beautiful and open. Mine. Holding myself above her with one hand, I guide my cock to her opening. With the tip seated in her heat, I rebalance over her and pause, perched on the edge, letting the anticipation build. She tilts her hips up a fraction, and I pin her in place with a small thrust. "Don't rush this, rabbit."

"I need you." Her voice is a husky whine. Rough from the screaming she's done each time we've come together over the past hours.

"Gotta savor you, baby." I shift forward, deeper, stretching her open. Each squeeze and flutter threatens to wreck my control and have me fucking her hard. Again. But this time will be slow, sweet, and satiating. I hope. Because I have to get out of this bed, even though I'm pretty sure I could die a happy man right here. Another inch. Her thighs hugging my hips, fingertips gripping my shoulders, puffs of breath teasing my chest, eyes nearly closed, trusting. She's got me tied up in knots, and I don't think I'll ever free myself. Why would I want to?

One final deep thrust, and I'm seated in the cradle of her hips. Fuck, there is nothing that has ever felt this good. I lower myself, to press my chest against hers, nuzzle her neck. Peach ice cream, melted on a hot summer day. The scent slips inside me, owning me. She wiggles the tiniest bit, trapped in my embrace, begging silently for more. I could tease and torture her, but the day is starting and I have to leave. No matter how much I want to, I can't linger inside her. Any more than I can tie her up.

She'd be so gorgeous with my ropes spun around her.

The image triggers me to move. I imagine her suspended, wrapped like a gift for me. Her juicy pussy at the perfect height to swing onto my dick, every move controlled by me. Her sweet cries of submission caressing my balls while she takes my length deep inside. Exactly as she's doing now. Deeper and deeper, until the press of my cock inside her chokes us both on the sensation of being united. Faster, losing control or letting it go. My grip on her hips mimics the scene in my head, holding her in place, moving her where she should be to take everything I'm giving. My back bows as I lose control. As I release, she cries out, going over with me, the rhythmic tug on my cock drawing out every last drop of my cum. I collapse but roll at the last moment so I don't crush her.

Words don't form, so I hold her tight against me until I can breathe regularly again. So I can string together a sentence. She's quiet. Too quiet. I scrape her hair back from her face and tilt her chin until she looks at me. "You okay, rabbit?"

"Too good." She closes her eyes and rests her forehead on my chest.

I hold her because I don't know what it means to be "too good," but it sounds like clouds gathering on a perfectly sunny day. Whatever it is, it will pop this bubble we've made. Anytime in my life I've been this content, it's been ripped away.

Fuck. What am I doing? She's probably worn out, and I'm making it into a big ole deal. "How about some breakfast?"

"Sounds good, but I need a shower first."

I smack her ass playfully. "Clean up. I'll grab one after I feed you. Meet me downstairs."

She moves out of my arms, and the bubble pops

anyway because that's what bubbles do. We still have another day before everyone comes back.

But first, I have to feed her and call Gabe. I slip on jeans and a shirt in case I decide to make bacon and grab my phone before jogging down the stairs with a goofy grin and a vague sense that she's right: we're too good.

"Gabe, I slept in," I say when he answers.

"Figured that out. Halfway suspected you'd taken the weekend off."

"No such luck. We gotta get that door installed." Hell, still gotta pick it up, and that takes a day.

"Talked them into delivering."

"What?"

"Their delivery guy has a run to Glenwood, so they called to see if I wanted delivery." Gabe pauses. "After you didn't answer your phone."

I look at my screen and check for missed calls. *Shit.* "Sorry about that."

"Lookin' forward to the story. Anyway, I'm leaving now so I can meet the guy. See you out there?"

"Yeah, I'll be right behind you."

Gabe's laughing when he hangs up. I'm the one who's usually early, calling him, pushing to start earlier and stay later. He knows something's up, but I'm not sure of how much of this story I should share. Probably none.

The eggs and bacon are in the fridge as Amy said. She even left a frying pan on the back burner of the stove. Like I can't find a pan. Three drawers later, I find the spatula. Bacon sizzling, I pull a couple of bagels from the freezer and shove them in the refrigerator for tomorrow. I haven't done the best job of keeping SJ fed. We split a sandwich and had some tortilla chips and salsa somewhere around midnight. Probably not enough to make up for the calories we burned. If it weren't for the need to finish the condo for Blake, we'd probably still be tearing up the sheets.

"Mmm. Bacon."

I spin to find her in the doorway of the kitchen. She's barefoot, in jeans and a form-fitting pink tee. Wet hair, so dark the red is nearly black, tied in a braid. Lookin' like all kinds of sexy country girl. Damn.

"Help yourself." I nod at the filled plate. "How do you like your eggs?"

"Fried or scrambled right in that pan of grease."

"Good girl." I crack four eggs directly into what's left of the fat I didn't already drain off. "Best way to make them."

She has a mouthful of meat but still manages to smile. The eggs don't take but a couple minutes. I plate it up. "Grab forks."

Unlike me, she goes straight for the silverware drawer like she lives here. A pang of "what if" follows that observation. Yeah. No. I put the plates on the table, on opposite sides. Gabe'll be waiting if I don't get a move on.

"What are your plans for today? Doing some writing?" Guilt about leaving her alone pushes my questions.

She sighs and sets down her fork. "I should be, but I'm stuck. I think I need time away from the story, to let it come to me."

I nod as if I know the first thing about writing a book.

"You?" Her tone is soft, barely a question.

We're not at the stage of accounting to each other, but I started this. "Soon as I'm done eating, heading to the resort to put in a fire door with Gabe."

"I'd love to see it."

"The door?"

"No, the resort, you goof."

I grin at her because I am goofy. Good sex does that to a person. "You can tag along. I'll give you a tour. But first, eat your breakfast."

She scoops up another bite of eggs. She's glowing; even her eyes are smiling.

I have no idea why I offered to take her with me except that I'm not ready to leave her alone. She fascinates me. More questions than answers. Wonder if I'll get a chance to figure her out before she heads back to Texas. The one place I can't follow her.

***

"OH MY GOD. THIS IS AMAZING." SJ is standing outside my truck, tracking from the first, mostly complete condo building to the restaurant and around the estate. "How big is it?"

"Big enough to satisfy." I nudge her shoulder and grab her hand.

"Was that a dick joke?" She bumps me back but lets me guide her to the entrance.

"Guess not, if you have to ask." Gabe's truck is in the lot. Hope the delivery guy didn't already get here. Or maybe I do so I can finish and take SJ back to the inn. Back to bed.

"Seriously, what all is planned for this place?"

"For now, finishing this first set of units, the restaurant, and the dungeon. Stone's planning on adding more multi-unit buildings like this one and some cottages out there." I point toward the wooded part of the property.

"You did all this?"

I laugh. "Not at all. We've had a ton of crews out there. Concrete guys, plumbers, electricians, framers, you name it. Gabe and I have been on-site for all of it. Overseeing, working, but there's no way two guys could have done this."

"Did you work on big sites like this in St. Louis?"

"Sometimes." I'm not okay talking about my past, leaving breadcrumbs back to my home. Habit I got into when I left Texas and one I'm not ready to change. The automatic door to the lobby glides back. I head directly to the huge, interconnected three-bedroom-two-bedroom condos we're finishing for Eliot and the other guys. Ground-floor access, fully wheelchair accessible with all the latest gadgets like voice-activated lights and environment controls. Inside the opening between the units is bare. No door.

I holler into the living area. "Gabe?"

"Back here."

SJ tries to free herself, but I tug her with me to the bedrooms. Gabe's in the primary with the en suite bath.

"Got the temp door off," he says from the ladder

where he's finished installing a lightbulb in the new fixture. "Test it."

"Lights on," I say. The fixture illuminates almost instantly.

SJ stares at the ceiling. "That is so cool."

"Think that's cool? Check out the shower controls." I guide her over the wet area. The tile continues straight in behind the glass wall, a variety of shower heads including rain and massage and side spouts breaking up the slate. "All controlled by this panel, which can save six presets. And if you slide the panel closed with this button," I point at the control for the freaking heavy shatterproof door that closes off the area, "it can be used as a steam room."

"I could die happy in here." SJ glances over to the jetted tub. "Seriously, I want to live in this bathroom." She plunks down on the built-in bench. "Send food."

I chuckle at her. "It's not even painted yet. Amy wouldn't let you move in until it's fully decorated." And I wouldn't let her live with the guys. I would keep her all to myself if she was staying. An image of her naked in the shower, taking my cock, comes to me clear as day. She is wrecking me. I step out of the shower and ask Gabe, "When's the door supposed to get here?"

He glances at his phone. "Half hour."

"Mind if we check out the restaurant?" I ask.

Gabe gives me a knowing look.

Yes, I mean the dungeon. Might be the only time I ever have a woman alone in one. "Unless you need help screwing in lightbulbs."

"I'll call you when it gets here."

"Want to see the rest?" I ask SJ.

She picks herself off the bench and comes to me. I take her hand again as soon as we leave the apartment. We start in the restaurant, with its huge windows designed to catch the sunset and the beautiful mountain views. Booths line the two solid walls, and tables fill in the open space. Wood rafters with oil-rubbed bronze fittings make the space feel intimate according to Amy. My favorite are the bronze chandeliers that look like antlers, despite the fact they were a bitch to install. SJ oohs and ahs and touches each detail within her reach.

I don't bother with the kitchen. "Let's go downstairs."

The slight hesitation before she agrees surprises me, but I blow it off. She's fascinated by the luxury space, probably wasn't ready to move on, but I can't wait to get her in the dungeon now that we're here. I take her down the stairs since we're still waiting for the elevator sign-off. It's a story and a half down. Plenty of space in between for soundproofing materials. SJ is quiet. I pause before I press the bar on the door. "You okay?"

"Yeah. Of course. Excited to see it."

I lean on the bar with my ass, keeping my eyes on her. Only a few steps back to trigger the motion lights and reveal the space. She turns her head away from me, to the open room, and gasps. Yeah. That's the reaction I was looking for. Pot lights run along the outer edges of the room, softly illuminating the privacy booths and some of the more static stations. There's a ton more lighting that took forever to install, all controlled by a central panel in the sound booth. A full stage fills the end of the long room, about where the kitchen is in the restaurant. Beams crisscross the ceiling, providing infinite points of attachment. My mandatory addition to the space. It was a huge expense and time-consuming but totally worth it in the end for the flexibility it will give us. SJ tugs free of me and walks to one of the leather panels that line the walls.

"It's padded." She glances back at me.

"Double duty. Soundproofing and a comfortable place to rest if you're restrained." I tilt my head to the ceiling.

Her mouth forms an O. She scampers over to one of the booths, trying it out before she bounces back up to check out some of the equipment we've already installed: spanking benches, St. Andrew's crosses, various stockades. She bends down to inspect one of the tables with a built-in cage.

"Wow.

"We have private rooms too. But those aren't set up yet. Waiting on paint before we put the furniture in."

She nods, eyes wide. This place is already completely different from Pandora, the only dungeon she's been in. As I open my mouth to ask her if she wants to see how the restraints work, my phone dings. Gabe, saving me from a bad decision.

I text back. *Be right there.*

"We gotta go. Door's here."

"I'll find somewhere to sit. A flood of ideas for the marketing copy hit me."

"Of course. Lobby has plenty of seating. You need a paper or pen?"

"Got my phone. I'll dictate."

Man, I'd love to get a copy of that recording.

I rush to help Gabe with the door. It's a heavy bastard. When we finally finish installing it and connecting the accessibility controls, Gabe reminds me it's a holiday weekend and we have to take some time off. If SJ wasn't here, or soon to be back in my bed, I'd argue with him. Instead, I wish him well and make plans to drive in together early on Tuesday.

⁂

AFTER ANOTHER NIGHT and most of the day feeding and fucking SJ, I'm almost completely at ease, one arm folded behind my head, the other around her, staring at the ceiling. There should be words after the weekend we've shared, but there's still a tiny disconnect between us, a distance that maybe my ropes could have closed. Maybe the unease is all me because I know she's leaving soon. "You okay?"

"Mmm-hmm."

"Hungry?"

"No, but I should probably take a shower. Everyone will be back soon."

Is she worried about being caught in bed with me?

Am I?

I'm the one who broke the easy silence.

She rolls to sit on the edge of the bed. "This was a fantastic weekend, Alex."

But...? I wait for her to say it, clenching my jaw tight so I don't say it first.

She sighs a shuddering breath. "But I think we should keep it to ourselves. Don't want everyone making more of this than it can be. I'm not staying."

"Not like you're leaving today, right?"

She glances back at me, her blue eyes cloudy. "No, but I *am* leaving. Soon."

I fake a shrug. "You have a book to write, and you saw all the work I have to do. Bright and early tomorrow. This was a nice break."

She nods. A smile teases her lips but doesn't quite appear. I expect her to say something else or at least plant a parting kiss on my lips. But she turns her head and walks out of my room. I rub my chest where my heart twinges as the door closes. I don't know her well enough to call this feeling love. Hell, I don't know her at all except how she sounds when she comes, and how her eyelids flutter with pleasure, and how her nails sting when she clutches my shoulders. I know every line of the butterfly tattoo on her back and how it looks ready to take flight when I sink into her again and again.

But I wouldn't know how to tell my mama about her, how to explain why I'm so captivated. In some ways, I've known more about the rope bunnies I've played with than I know about SJ. She's a BDSM romance writer from Texas with an asshole agent. And I can't let her tie me in knots.

Maybe we'll hook up a couple more times, a way to get her out of my system before she goes. In the meantime, she has a book and I have a resort to finish.

I leave the bed, strip the sheets, and take a shower. My hair's still wet and I'm tucking the last pillow into the fresh case when Amy and Tyler and the rest of the gang bust inside downstairs, talking and laughing. I toss the pillow on my bed and head downstairs. Alone.

FOURTEEN

SJ

Alex is back to his early morning-late night routine. I press back and up into downward dog, letting the sunshine warm my back. An echo of an ache lingers between my thighs. The ache isn't real. It's been too long for my muscles to still be strained. The ache is a manifestation of missing him. I keep moving through my routine as the sun moves lower in the sky. As I finish in mountain pose, I sense eyes on me. The windows reflect the sunset, so I can't tell where it's coming from. But I know who it must be. He's nowhere to be found after I roll up my mat and head inside. His avoidance, or absence, or whatever is keeping him hidden is making me crazy.

I take a shower and try to write, but my mind won't focus. My characters won't spend time together. It's impossible to write a romance when the characters won't enter the same room. With that realization, a plan forms.

It's not time yet—a couple more hours, and then I can flip the page on this story. I distract myself with more videos of lovers with ropes, but I don't get myself off. The pressure builds.

Darkness fills the hallway, everyone long since retired to their respective rooms. I dart to Alex's room on my tiptoes. His door is unlocked. Did he expect me? Hope I would sneak in? I slip inside before the light from his bathroom can spill into the hall. With my back pressed against the door, I flip the lock. He comes out fresh from a shower, towel on his head rubbing his short hair dry.

The moment he becomes aware of me, he halts. "Whatcha' doing, little rabbit?"

"Miss you. Can't sleep."

His cock responds, twitching and lengthening.

My straps on my simple cotton nightgown easily shift down my arms as I pull the fabric free of my body.

"Fuck." It's a whisper, a prayer, and a curse all rolled into one. And the word slithers between my thighs bringing heat and priming me for exactly what he can give me.

I raise my arms up, cross my wrists, and step wide. "Yes, please."

He's on his knees, face buried in my core before I can move again. He grips my knee, lifting my leg over his shoulder. When he follows up with my other leg, I'm completely at his mercy. His tongue dances through my folds, and my body electrifies with need. My nerves are primed to react to him. Somehow, he lifts me, and I drop my hands to his shoulders, his tongue deep in my folds. He doesn't stop until he drops me on the bed.

"You're mine, little rabbit."

I nod and quickly follow with "Yes." I don't want to be chastised for not using my words when there are so much better uses for his mouth.

He moves me where he wants and resumes giving me the best oral sex I've ever had, holding my thighs wide apart. Sucking my clit, scissoring his fingers inside, stretching me. There's nowhere to hide from him. I don't want to.

My brain clouds with pleasure. I'm shaking, flutters from my insides riding over my entire body. With a gasp, the waves roll over me, and I'm lost. His mouth is on mine, swallowing my moans. I suck his tongue the way he sucked me. He lifts my back from the bed so he can wrap me in his embrace, holding me tight, bracing on his forearms. His legs squeeze mine together. I can't move, only feel him. His hard length pressed along my stomach, my breasts pressed to his chest, and his lips making love to mine. He doesn't need ropes to capture me, but I need more. The word spoken against his lips is more breath than vocalization.

He lifts his head. His eyes are smoldering and dark in the dim light. He's the trouble I've always been attracted to. I shiver with the irrational, inadvisable craving for him.

"Don't move." His gaze bores into me.

I go completely lax in his hold. "Okay." I swallow the edgy taste of risk that being with him brings. I can't help it. I can't fully believe it. I can't wait for him to be inside me again.

He's off the bed, in the bathroom, reappearing in seconds rolling on a condom. "Good little rabbit."

His praise washes over me as soothing as a warm bath, as warm as a fire, as delicious as a fine meal. Again, he rearranges my limbs the way he wants them. My ass is resting on his bent knees where he crawled up on the mattress. My thighs cradle his hips, and his cock kisses my entrance.

"Please, Alex." If he doesn't press inside me now, I'm going to lose my mind.

With a subtle shift, his cock breaches me ever so slightly. Even with my orgasm and his preparation with his fingers, the press is an invasion, a conquering, a sweet hint of what's to come. Does he want me to beg? I will. I'm ready to cry for him to fuck me. To get deep inside where he was for an entire weekend, where he's been absent for far too many days. Deeper. So slowly he presses inside, drawing parts of my body toward him like I'm a puppet on his strings. I dig my toes into the mattress, seeking him, inviting him, silently pleading for all of him. His fingers dig into my hips, controlling me. I surrender, and he takes me over. His cock so deep, his balls are on my ass.

We both pant a few breaths. I search for the peace that will keep me from falling over the edge too quickly. I waited so long to be back here. Denied myself what I most needed. Him. He folds forward, plants a kiss on my lips. "I'm going to fuck you now. Deep and hard until you want to scream. Until you come all over my cock. Until I fucking explode inside you."

I clench my pelvis muscles, teasing him the way his words tease me. He nips the hard bead of my breast and then proceeds to do exactly as he promised. Clutching my hips, he pounds in and out of me, no mercy. No retreat. Exactly what I hoped for when I snuck in his room.

I'm completely lost when he pulls out and flips me over. A mewl of protest squeaks out before I lose my breath as he plunges back inside. He's so deep he's in my throat, or he would be if that was possible. Hard. Fast. Deep. Over and over again, he gives me everything. I press my mouth to the pillow and muffle the sounds of my body coming apart. He clamps his hands tighter to my hips, up on his knees, back arched, he shudders his cum into the condom, and part of me wishes he was coating my walls. Crazy. The man makes me absolutely insane with need and poor judgement. He's my drug of choice and probably as bad for me as any drug could be. Or maybe I'm the toxic one. I can't figure it out as he leaves my body, disappears into the bathroom, only to reappear and wrap me in his arms.

"Sleep, little rabbit."

And I do. For a few hours before I free myself and return to my room. He probably woke up, but he didn't stop me. I guess that says more than words could

The next morning, he's gone before daylight hits the mountaintop. His avoidance saddens me. But I asked for distance and reinforced my request by leaving his room. Do I deserve to feel anything except shame?

I return to my writing routine but resist writing any conflict between my hero and heroine, despite all the advice articles telling me conflict is the key to fiction. One of the books on plotting romance insists that there is a third act breakup. I don't want to break my characters up. I barely got them together. They finally like each other; they have nothing to fight about. Maybe I can use some external force, like a tornado or terrorist attack, to rip them apart. Something outside their control that won't make them be terrible to each other. Because I'm being terrible to Alex, and it sours my stomach and keeps me from sleeping. I'm supposed to be getting dirt on him to help my uncle take him down. And I'm letting my uncle down because I can't do it.

Maybe my real-life story needs what my fiction required. Research. I pick up my phone, walk out to the patio so no one in the inn will overhear my conversation, and call my cousin, Alyss.

The line rings twice, and then the odd accent of west Texas and refined Charleston combined is calling out my name. "Sarah Jane. How are you, cousin?"

"I'm good. In Colorado for a bit of a working vacation. How are you?" We haven't talked in months, maybe even a year. Our relationship has narrowed down to social media and liking and commenting on each other's posts. Distant but kind of connected. "How are those babies?"

"They aren't babies anymore. Liam starts kinder-garten this fall."

Alyss married a doctor six or seven years ago. She asked me to be her maid of honor, but I didn't have any money and didn't want her future husband's charity. I had more pride then. I ask her more questions about her family and how she's doing being a stay-at-home mom. She seems happy.

"So I'm writing a book. A romance."

The pause before her response makes me a little nervous. "Romance?"

I force a tiny laugh. "Yeah, a sexy story. But I was wondering if you could help me with it."

"Me?" Is that suspicion in her tone. "I read cozy mysteries or parenting books." She laughs nervously, as if someone might be recording our conversation or watching over her shoulder.

"Do you remember that cowboy you dated in high school? The tall blond?"

She sucks in a breath. "Alex?"

"Yeah, Alex *Craig*?"

"Why would you ask about him?"

Shit, it's the right Alex. "Oh. I just thought you might be able to help me. I need some conflict in my story, and I remember your dad was upset you were dating. Kind of pulled you two apart. Something about being caught in a barn?"

"That was the worst day of my life. I spent a lot of time getting over it. I love the life I have now. I love my husband. Talking about an old boyfriend... It's not something I can revisit. I'm sorry."

"That's okay." I'm not sure what else to say.

"Sarah Jane, I'm so sorry, I have to run. The baby woke up, and he's crying."

"Of course. Love you."

"You too. We'll talk soon."

The call ends, and I stare at the screen for a few minutes. I play the conversation over in my head, trying to figure out why Alyss would be so resistant if she's completely over Alex. Unless Alex did hurt her. Amy appears in my path, disrupting my circular thoughts.

"Do you have plans for lunch? I mean, obviously writing, but would you have time to take a break?"

"Sure?" Amy seems overly excited about a sandwich. "Need help in the kitchen?"

She laughs. "No, I'm having lunch with Katherine in town. Gabe's wife?" She shakes her head. "We meet occasionally and always end up talking about books, and since you're a writer, I thought..."

"I'd love to." Because while I'm not a real writer yet, I want to be. I've fallen in love with this book. And the urge to talk about it all the time is crazy strong. The call with Alyss was supposed to do double duty—talk about my book and Alex. Too bad she shut me down. "What time?"

"Leave in about an hour?"

"I'll freshen up and meet you down here." As I'm rushing up the stairs to my room, it occurs to me that I haven't gone out with girlfriends in forever. Lunch with

Amy and Katherine takes on new significance, an importance my closet is not supporting. The empty hangers clang when I smash my shirts to the side and flip through them again, one at a time. Nothing. I tip my chin and check my outfit. Solid blue knit shirt that brings out my eyes and shows off my cleavage. Good enough. In the bathroom, I touch up my makeup and comb the ends of my hair. Not exactly famous author worthy, but I'm not famous, or an author, so it doesn't matter.

FIFTEEN

SJ

Amy takes me to the same place in town I ate at before, the Stone Bear. It's a few doors away from the hardware store. My cheeks heat at the memory of showing the clothesline to Alex. *Alex.* Could I sneak into his room again tonight? He'll probably start locking his door now, and how embarrassing would it be to be caught in the hallway like that? Maybe he'll sneak into mine?

Katherine is tall and thin and gorgeous. She's older than me, with a subtle New York accent, and could have easily been a model. I'm a little in awe of her and the way she fills a room, even a restaurant-sized one. But her smile seems genuine when she meets me.

"I ordered wine. You drink, right?"

Amy laughs. "This is SJ. She writes romance."

Katherine's warm smile is welcome after my cousin's response to my confession.

I return the gesture and tell her, "I'd love a glass of wine."

I settle into a chair between them. They chat about the resort construction. Amy told me Katherine is married to Gabe, that man I met who works with Alex. He seems younger than her, and her face lights up like she can't hold in her happiness when she talks about him. I ignore the twinge of jealousy that both Amy and Katherine have their dream men.

"So do you have any kids?" Amy asks.

Is she talking to me?

"Not at the moment," Katherine responds. "Probably around the holiday. Seems to be a tense time for families." Katherine sips her wine while I try to figure out what she's talking about.

"Katherine and Gabe foster."

"Oh. Wow. That's got to be a lot." I'm at a loss for words, not having met a foster parent before. She seems like she belongs in Aspen, not taking care of someone else's kids in crisis.

"I love it."

The food comes and interrupts whatever else she might have said.

My Asian-inspired salad is delicious, and I dig in after a tentative bite, suddenly starved.

"What are you reading?" Katherine asks Amy.

Amy turns pink. "Um. I kind of fell into a series about orcs."

"Orcs? Like the green goblin monsters with tusks?"

"That's the one." Amy shrugs.

Katherine laughs. "Oh my. Tell me more, because if it makes *you* blush like that, I have to read it."

"Them. It's a series."

"Spill," Katherine commands, and Amy does.

I follow the conversation while I try to keep from laughing salad out my nose and the description of the monster cocks and quantity of cum these guys have.

"Damn, I need a shower," I blurt.

"I know. Hot, right?"

"Sticky. Imaging all that..." I wave my hand around my body. "Makes me want to wash."

After we catch our breath, Katherine asks the dreaded question. "So what do you write?"

It's easier to answer after talking about orc peen. "Romance. Erotic romance."

Katherine leans forward. "Really." She drags the word out. "Tell me more."

I rattle on for a bit about my work in progress.

"I'm intrigued. What's your author name?"

I consider picking another author's name for the briefest moment to cover my uncle's lies, but I can't bring myself to take credit for someone else's hard work. "I'm sorry, I despite my...agent's enthusiasm, I haven't published yet. I'm not sure what name I'll use."

Katherine leans closer to me. "Give me your phone." I hand it over when I probably should have questioned her. She adds herself as a contact. "Promise once you do decide, you'll share that secret name so I can brag that I know an author."

I chuckle and nod, tucking my phone away, but don't

promise because I can't. I glance over at Amy, but if she was shocked by my confession, her face shows nothing.

Katherine changes the subject to chat about a hot regency romance series she's been reading with spanking. Amy writes the name and title down eagerly. Having seen her get spanked in person, it makes sense she'd want to read about it.

Lunch lasts for two hours, and I'm more relaxed and happier than I can remember being except for the weekend with Alex. My contentment doesn't last. Right as we get to the inn, my phone rings.

"Excuse me," I tell Amy. "I have to take this. It's my agent." Another lie, but it's not a new one, simply a repeat of the original lie my uncle told before I got here. Each phone call gets more and more uncomfortable, but he's supporting my writing career, so I answer.

"What the hell are you doing out there, girly?"

Still walking away from the car, down the block so I'm not overheard, I ask, "What do you mean?"

"It's been six weeks. That fancy inn ain't cheap. Did you get any dirt on Alex or not?"

"There's nothing to find."

"Bullshit. You aren't trying. Should I have been like you and given up when you were being treated like a whore in California? Should I have left you there? Of course not. Because that's not what family does. We take care of each other, right?"

I want to agree, but something about what Alyss didn't say niggles at the back of my brain. "What happened? That day in the barn with Alyss?"

"She disappeared right after Alex's graduation ceremony. I knew in my gut something wasn't right. I searched everywhere, finally found them in the barn. He had her tied up. Taking advantage of her. She was underage. He left her humiliated and broke our family. She couldn't even finish her senior year. He ruined us with what he forced her to do."

My salad rises in my throat at the image, the accusation.

"You should know all about being forced to do things. Or don't you remember?"

I remember all too well, and I can't speak with the horrible images he's bringing to mind.

"You know, if you forgot, I got some pictures of my own. Took them when I found them. Be a real shame if they ended up on the internet. Maybe I'll send you a couple by email so you can remember what I saved you from. Remember you owe me."

"What?" Pictures? He took pictures of me? My heart seizes as if I've been stabbed.

"I didn't send you out there to take a damn vacation."

"I thought it was to write my book." I look for a place to sit because my legs aren't going to hold me.

"You can write whatever you want, but I want dirt on Alex Craig. I think you can figure out what happens if you fail."

The pictures of me being abused get released.

I hate this man.

Guilt rushes in. He was the one who searched for me in California. He was the one who got me free. But he's also the one who's holding explicit photos over my head, pressuring me to take down a man who's supposed to be terrible but has been nothing but nice—loving, even. I don't know what happened ten years ago, but Alyss didn't accuse Alex of ruining her life, only said it was the worst day of her life.

Was that because of Alex or Uncle MD?

"You're gonna owe me for all the expenses, the plane flight, the Sunflower—all of it—if you don't deliver."

Without a job, there's no way I can pay my uncle back. He'd have to sue me, but that would create more bad blood in the family, and Alyss and I barely speak now. "I'll keep trying, but he hasn't done anything wrong. Won't do anything wrong. I called Alyss. She didn't want to say what happened."

"It was a traumatic event for her. She probably got some PTSD or something from it. Or she's lying because she don't want to tell you about it. I bet she'd remember quick if I told her you were living with him."

My steps falter. He wouldn't. Except he would. I don't have a lot of family. And while we've drifted apart, Alyss is my cousin, was my best friend. The fact I can call her anytime is a safety net. My aunt too. I have a place to spend the holidays if I wanted to. He could easily break my relationship with them. No more quickly than Alyss finding out I slept with her old boyfriend. How did I get myself into this?

An offer I couldn't refuse and a threat I can't avoid. Pictures of me being forced to do—

My throat tightens, and bile rises up from my guts.

They can't be made public. I wouldn't know how to live if that happened.

"I did find out he was living in St. Louis before this." Guilt washes over me as soon as the words leave my lips.

"That's good. I can search the records there. But I need more. He's got to be caught red-handed to get that predator off the streets."

If I do this, am I the monster or is he? "I'll be able to get what you need if you give me more time."

"How much?"

I don't know. Forever? Never? "A month?"

He barks a bitter laugh.

"Two weeks, then? Their new club is opening, and I'll be able to make something happen by then. I promise." Like find a way out of this?

"You better get me something, or these pictures are going to find their way to your momma, your old boss, and everyone on the internet." He ends the call.

In my email, there's a new message. I open it with shaking hands. The attachment is slow to load. But when it does, I have to look away and fight to keep my lunch down. I'm not sure whose dick is shoved down my mouth. Their face isn't visible, but mine is. The tears, the mussed hair, the runny makeup aren't enough to conceal my identity. There's a second attachment, but I can't make myself open it.

The walk back to the inn is dreadful, each step taking me closer to a task I shouldn't have agreed to and there isn't an escape from. Unless I want to be ruined forever, unable to get a job because those images will be on the internet and associated with my name. And I'd have to give up any connection to what little remains of my family.

There's no other option, I have to find a way to catch Alex being the predator my uncle swears he is.

I'll hate myself for doing it, but self-preservation is a powerful motivator.

Exhausted and sick to my stomach, I drag myself up to my room and fall down on the bed, too tired to even cry.

SIXTEEN

ALEX

A tap, tap, tap at my door rouses me from the almost sleep I'd fallen into. My muscles ache as I drag myself from my bed. There's a week until the opening. I'm working around the clock to try to finish along with Gabe and all the subs. We're so close.

I open the door.

SJ.

My body comes alive as if I've been on vacation and slept ten hours.

"Can I come in?" she asks in a low voice. She shoots a furtive glance down the hall.

I peek out into the empty space, too, tug her inside, and close the door quietly. The lock is loud when it snicks closed. I've been aching to be with her again, another stolen moment before she leaves for good. I probably should have been the one to sneak into her room, but the days have zoomed by and the only thing that matters is getting the resort done for the opening. At least, that's what I want to believe.

She flings her arms around my shoulders, lifts to her tiptoes, and kisses me, her breasts pressed against my bare chest. Having SJ back in my arms, I recognize the lies I've been telling myself. This warm, sexy woman matters a whole lot.

Fuck. Her kisses are so dang sweet. I'm torn between clutching her closer and ripping her clothes off. Bare breasts win. Still kissing, I lift the hem of her shirt. It bunches up. She breaks the kiss and helps me free her. No bra. I groan my approval, bend my knees, and suckle one tender bud. She drops her shirt and arches into my mouth.

"Missed you," I mumble before moving my attention to the other side.

She runs her fingers through my hair. "Missed you too. And I wanted to ask you something."

Her face, filled with unease, pauses the sexy times, and I stand. "Anything."

She twists a finger into her own gorgeous red hair and freezes, dropping her hands. "Would you be my date to the opening?"

Her words twist around my heart, squeezing it. "Yes, ma'am." I clear the feels out of my throat and caress her cheek with my thumb. "I'd be honored to be your date."

I kiss her to seal the deal. Her fingers find their way between me and my sleep pants, and all thoughts of openings and dates disappear like smoke. I follow her lead and shove the hem of her yoga pants down. *Fuck me.* No panties either. The fabric glides down her legs, and I follow to my knees. The seductive scent of her arousal calls to me. She lifts one dainty foot, then the other, as I bare her.

The pants go flying, my hands grip her ass, and I nudge my shoulder between her legs. I have to taste her again, bury my tongue in her silky hole. I lap at her folds, savoring her unique salty sugar. She moans, and I nearly lose my hold on her as she tilts back to give me more access. Shifting her to the bed, I open her legs wide, duck down, and let the back of her knees rest on my shoulders. A passing buzz that I shouldn't be alone with her flits by, and I swat the thought away like a pesky mosquito. It's an echo of an old fear and there's only so many more days I might have with her.

I sip and savor her, sucking her clit, until she's writhing in my arms, still quiet, like we're teenagers that might get caught. I falter at that unwelcome image. She lifts her head to peer down at me, a question on her face. She ain't no virgin, and I ain't no schoolboy. I return to the task of making her fly apart in my arms, and she does. Soft keening cries escape her lips, despite her efforts to be quiet.

Yeah, baby. I got you. I slip on one of the last condoms from the box I stole from Cade. Might have to steal the box I bought him as a replacement too. She helps me roll it down. Her touch makes me shiver and twitch. I got it bad for this woman. Maybe she can stay out here permanently.

I notch the tip of my dick at her hot, swollen entrance. Maybe she could stay with me.

With a shift of my hips, I sink slowly into her welcoming heat. It's like going home for the holidays—it feels like I belong. A few more slow thrusts, and I'm as deep as I can get into heaven. For a moment, I linger, letting our connection build. Her fingers dig into my back, and she twitches her hips. Little rabbit teases me to move. With a predatory grin, I give her what she silently requested. More, faster, harder. Her breathy pants from when we had the inn to ourselves reverberate in my brain, and I move to that rhythm. The one she taught me.

She shifts back on the mattress, riding the tidal wave I'm creating. I follow her, climbing up to follow her one leg at a time, angling her, moving her exactly where she should be. So much easier with ropes. I glance to the closet where I have them hanging loose. Wouldn't be a moment to grab one and go to work. But I'd have to leave this silky haven, and that ain't happening. Not even for a minute. Not even to make it better because it's damn fine already. Best ever.

I brush the hair back from her forehead so I can focus on her beautiful eyes. She blinks up at me, locked in the moment until she bites her lip and glances away. I'm too intense. It's too soon for what I'm feeling for her, so I bottle it up and focus on the task at hand. Giving her more pleasure than anyone has gifted her before. Making sure that even if she does leave, she'll be back, searching for what we have. Carving myself into her soul like someone inked that butterfly into her skin.

She wraps her legs around my hips, tying me deep inside. With a flick of my hips, I flip us so she's on top, can take what she wants without working so hard. Gives me a chance to finger her the way she needs. She's riding me so good, breasts bouncing, hands tugging her hair up and away. She's a fucking spread in a magazine, and I'm the only lucky fucker who can see her like this. There's a moment when my cock tells me to turn her again, take her from behind and own her, but I ignore the urge.

She's too beautiful right where she is.

Her body freezes, head tilted to the ceiling, eyes closed. *Now.* I press hard on her magic button, adding the pressure she likes, and she goes off like a storm. Her thighs, her pussy, her hands—everything is squeezing me as she releases a flood over my dick. As soon as she softens, I roll us again and pound into her wet heat a few more times before I unload into the condom so hard I should be worried about breaking it. The last bit of cum jerks out of my tip, and I fall to the side. The exhaustion from the day rolls over me like a wave, taking me down. With a quick swipe, I grab a couple tissues and manage to get the condom wrapped up. Not the best, but it will do for now. Because there's no way I can keep my eyes open for a minute longer.

My alarm rocks me from my sex coma, and I roll over to shut it off. I open my mouth to apologize to SJ for getting up so early, but...

She's gone.

IT'S DONE. Phase one of the resort is basically complete, and the restaurant looks star-spangled. Everything gleams, floor-to-ceiling windows showcasing the beautiful mountain view, servers working the room with fancy small food and drinks both virgin and spiked. Everyone is here: Gabe and Katherine, Amy and Tyler, and a bunch of people from our old club all dressed up and bunched in clusters chatting. A tall man with dark hair and trim beard stands next to Blake, who is the only one not smiling, but all the accommodations we made for his mobility worked flawlessly. Eliot and Cade are working the door, checking invitations against the list.

SJ slips her fingers into my hand, and I guide her over to our group. I glance around. "Where's Reed?"

Blake tilts his head back to scowl at me. "He had to fly back. Some emergency with closing on the house."

The guys share a business, property, and everything else. I'm not sure if they have more than one to sell, and Blake doesn't seem to be in a talkative mood. Instead of pushing him to engage, I address the man beside him. "Alex Craig."

He clasps my outstretched hand. "Simon St. James."

His accent sounds British.

"Nice to meet you." Blake should be doing the introductions, but he's too busy being pissed off about who knows what. Well, besides the obvious wheelchair thing. But fuck, bro, you're alive and at a club.

Not about to go there with him.

"I'm Mr. Foster's attorney."

I glance at Blake to see what he thinks about being

called "Mr. Foster." He's staring out one of the windows, ignoring us.

"Right," I say to the lawyer. Eliot had mentioned they were suing for damages and long-term care costs. This is not a conversation to have here and now. "This is SJ Reading."

Simon's eyes spark as he greets her. I almost didn't think she'd keep our date after she left me alone in bed, but I couldn't imagine being at the event with her not officially attached to me. My inner redneck would have chafed on that one. The fact that she looks incredible only would have stung more. Her clingy blue dress makes her eyes stand out even more than they usually do. I'll take it off her as soon as I can.

She insisted before we came tonight that, as my date, I would do a rope scene with her. It was a no brainer to agree, but I'm not ready to share her, not publicly. The private room is reserved. I glance around the restaurant, which I've spent so much time in while it was being built, is empty but moving toward this. Somehow seeing it serving the intended function disconnects me. It's no longer mine. It's the chef's room and the resort's main dining venue. It belongs to the guests.

Stone is talking to Delilah Rosen, the architect. She smiles at me as I approach with SJ in tow. There's an urge to turn and run. Working with her has been...challenging. But in the end, she was right about almost everything.

"Nice job on the details, Alex." She's dressed in a shiny red dress and matching spike heels. There's no doubt she'd spank my ass if she was unhappy with any of it. Stone would probably let her, or at least hold me down.

"Glad you approve. Looking forward to working on the next phase with you." That's an exaggeration born from my Southern manners. "Mind if I steal Stone away for a moment?"

Stone doesn't wait for her to answer. He excuses himself and moves SJ and me to a quiet corner. "What's up?"

I glance at SJ. Part of me would rather do this without all the proper forms, but no. With a deep breath in, I rush through my request. "Have a room reserved to do a scene. Need a consent form for SJ."

"Follow me." We head to the bar. "Cassie?"

The young curvy bartender we met at Pandora darts over to Stone. "Sir?"

She calls Stone "sir"? After a brief, inaudible exchange, she grabs a clipboard and hands it to him. He hands it to me. "Sit. Talk. Fill this out. I'll send Pierce over to witness your signature, SJ."

I nod and take a step.

"You cool with Cade and me as spotters?" Stone asks. Hadn't considered needing that, but the downstairs isn't fully staffed with dungeon masters or any other staff.

"Inside or outside?" I ask.

"Outside. Door unlocked, audio on." Stone can listen in on wireless earbuds.

"That works," I say. Stone doesn't move, his gaze boring into SJ.

She nods, but Stone doesn't move a muscle.

"Yes, sir," she says, and he nods approvingly.

Fuck. He's a total Dom. I'm an alpha, love to top my rope bunnies, but he's something else entirely.

Sitting in a booth, we review what I'm going to do with my ropes and the suspension.

"We need safe words. You cool with red, yellow, green?"

"Sure."

I have doubts whether she'd use them. A hint of doubt hits the back of my neck. Have to be extra cautious with checking the tension and keeping her talking. "I might not take you off the ground. It has to feel right to me." Despite her wanting that, me wanting that, that doubt has me warning her. "And any sexual interaction isn't guaranteed. Both of us have to be okay with it. Whatever we talk about, agree to now, the consent can be revoked."

She finally looks at me and nods. "I understand. I want this, Alex. I've been asking you to do this since we first got together."

I've resisted, despite wanting her wrapped up and under my control so badly. It's leftover worry from what went wrong back in that hay barn. It's been years. Time to get over it. SJ isn't Alyss. Despite the lingering doubt and the seriousness of the negotiation, I'm still excited to see what works with her body, test her flexibility—which should be good with all the yoga she does.

"Where do I sign?" she asks, seemingly as excited as I am to start the scene.

"Hold up." Pierce has to be here first. Finally, I spot

him working his way through the crowd, several people from Pandora stopping him, probably to say hi and comment on the new club. When he gets to us, he asks if we're ready. I hand him the paper. He takes his time, looking it over. "Any questions or concerns?"

The question is for SJ, not me. I hold my breath because she could back out.

"No."

"Safe words?"

She rattles off the stoplight list. He hands her the paper, and she signs it. Pierce signs it as a witness. It's not a contract or anything, so I don't sign it. In fact, I don't think I've used anything like this since I first started playing. And I wouldn't have asked for one with SJ, but with the new club, the new insurance, and a mix of nonmembers, the guys decided any private rooms used tonight had to have one in place. We'll check all the security we added after the event and make sure we can retrieve audio/video security footage if needed. This is a dry run of all the systems.

I'm not worried at all about the tech. Blake designed it, and Eliot oversaw the installation. But as the saying goes: trust but verify.

SEVENTEEN

ALEX

Cade and Stone follow us onto the elevator. It's nothing like the Box. Mirrors and polished wood. Soft lighting, no thumping music. At least not yet. The night has barely begun. We're the first couple to move downstairs, but I couldn't wait.

"Hold up." I release SJ's hand and duck into the men's locker room. My bag is in one of the lockers, stowed away in anticipation. I leave my shirt and boots and return to the group dressed, or *undressed*, for play.

When we get to the door of the room, my palms are sweaty and I have to rub my hand on my dark jeans before I can turn the knob. "Ready?"

SJ nods.

I wait.

"Yes."

I turn the handle and swing it wide. The lights turn on, showing off the square room with leather straps and chains limp against polished plaster walls a color between midnight and espresso. Bars and rings float down from the ceiling, crisscrossed with black painted beams that disappear in the black painted background. There are points of attachment scattered around the room to give maximum flexibility for scenes. The stained concrete floor is swirled in a similar dark cloud with shots of acid green and eggplant purple, according to the guys who did the staining. When they told me what they were doing, I wasn't too sure about it. But it's perfect to show off SJ's blue dress and red hair. She's the beautiful bird, and I'm about to put her in my cage.

Cade is in the hall handing Stone the earbuds.

"Test. Stone, can you hear this?" I say at a normal tone.

He gives me a thumbs-up and closes the door.

SJ jumps.

I drop my bag and approach her. I run my hands down her shoulders and gaze into her wary eyes. "Okay?"

"Yeah. Didn't expect chains."

I guide her toward the padded mats in the middle of the room.

"We're not using those. I'll use a ring, maybe two. But first, we're gonna get you relaxed, beautiful." I keep rubbing her shoulders down her arms until she settles into a soft, relaxed posture and breathing pattern. "There we go." I kneel and help her remove her matching blue heels. The suede is soft in my hands. I stand and place them under a padded bench in the corner. She doesn't move, her eyes following me. A single pull at the end of the bow that holds her dress together, and it slips apart. "Can I take off your dress?"

"Yes."

I part the sides of the fabric revealing the body I've spent hours worshiping and nights dreaming of. She's wearing a smooth black bra and matching panties; nothing fancy but silky smooth. No wonder there were no lines under her dress. I'd half expected her to be naked underneath. She shivers as I slip her arms free. I could tell her to fold it and place it on the bench, but I want to care for her, cherish her. After carefully laying it out so it won't be wrinkled later, I return and hold her shoulders the same way I did when we started. Slowly, I move my hands up and down her arms, lifting each of her hands and kissing her knuckles. I check her for any bruises or scratches. Anything that could cause her pain if I placed a rope in that spot. Her skin is creamy smooth with the faintest splash of freckles barely visible in the warm lighting. If we were somewhere else, I could spend hours tracing a path between them with my tongue. "I'm going to tie your hair."

She nods.

"Words."

"Please tie my hair, Alex."

I grab one of my shorter ropes, loop it around my fingers and stroke the fiery red strands into a ponytail. I tighten the loop, and she tips her head. One more wrap, and I use the strands to guide her to me. Her skin is soft and warm against mine. The pulse in her neck flutters; my little rabbit is nervous. Using the rope, I expose her neck. Her breath comes in pants, and her eyes are wide. I slip my free hand between her arm and her chest, up until I can clutch the front of her neck—not choking, holding. She's wrapped in my arms, under my control, and I wait until she calms into my care. Finally, her breath slows, and she relaxes. "There you go, little rabbit. I got you."

The kisses I place on her taut skin reinforce my praise, and she softens even more. The scent of her peachy skin is as soft and seductive as she is. It fogs my brain. With a deep breath, I unwrap my fingers from her neck, trailing them down her chest, over the clasp of her bra between her breasts. I pause, teasing her a little.

A few steps forward, and we're on the pads, centered under the rings that dangle from the ceiling. Rings I personally secured to a cross beam during construction. One of them could hold three times her weight easily. No limits to what I can do. As long as she agrees.

"Can I take off your bra?"

"Yes, please." Her blues eyes are filled with burning need. She looks like a goddess that I get to undress and then reclothe in my ropes, my ownership, my embrace.

I flick the front clasp open and peel back the sides. Her nipples are cool when I draw each one into my mouth, kissing and teasing the hardening buds with my tongue. She moans and arches into me. I tug the rope in her hair gently, adding to her pleasure based on the sounds she makes. Yeah, she's my little rabbit.

I could feast on her chest, but I promised to tie her. I *want* to tie her. So I place her bra with her dress and pull several more lengths of rope from my bag. I drop all but one bundle in arms' reach and snap one loose, drawing the length through my hands, fitting the ends together evenly, running back to the bite. The friction of the jute centers me, like a meditation.

Guiding the bite down her neck in a caress, she shivers. First, I'll create a harness around her chest. Her arms fold easily behind her back, so flexible. The ropes extend and enhance the embrace of my arms, offering a continuous comforting squeeze, the beautiful caress of her body in the layers of lines I lay down flat against her skin. Each line presses into her skin the way I want to press myself deep into her body. Each knot adds stability. I control the tension, taking her to the edge of discomfort but not crossing the line for her first time. Exploring the boundaries of her submission and pleasure. Finding the perfect balance.

She lets me turn her and move her limbs, lax and trusting. With the central knot in my hand, I hold her, matching our breaths, drawing the moment out so we both can feel the connection. Her shoulders are soft and relaxed as I draw my hands down her arms. "So beautiful, my sweet, sexy rabbit."

I clip the first carabiner to her harness, letting the weight rest on her breastbone. She freezes. "Breathe," I whisper in her ear. Tethered to me by the grip I have on the rope in her hair, I pick up another bundle of rope.

The new line draws easily through the ring. I'm not ready to suspend her, but soon.

On my knees, I take another bundle and pull it free,

presenting it to her like the queen she is before I wrap her hips snuggly. I could lift her from the chest harness, but not for her first time. This time, I'll have her completely cocooned. Completely at ease. Completely mine. I press a kiss to her stomach, below her belly button, before tightening my line against her pussy, parting her still covered lips, applying pressure exactly where she needs to associate my ropes with unlimited pleasure. A few more wraps, knots, and double checks of the tension and lead line, and I'm ready. I clip a second carabiner to her, the minimal weight pressing the rope to her clit enough for her to notice, based on her breathing.

I run my hands up her body, over my ropes, checking and touching. Evaluating the color of her skin, the pressure of the ropes, the pace of her breaths, the beat of her pulse. I connect her to my lead line. She's my entire world at this moment. Time has no meaning. There is only her, us, now. "Ready, little rabbit?"

"Yes, Alex."

With an easy draw of my line, she rises, floating in the air, wrapped in layers of my ropes. Every limb exactly where I placed it. Her face is completely relaxed, eyes half closed, safe under my control.

"Good girl."

She lifts her heavy gaze. "More."

I grip the line in her hair, and her eyes widen for me. "More what, little rabbit?"

"More you. I need you, Alex. I need you in me. Please, let me have you in my pussy. In my mouth. Somewhere."

Ah hell. My semihard cock goes fully erect behind my zipper. The ropes make her a horny bunny. And her needy begging has me in knots. She's perfect for me. "Left your panties on for a reason."

"But Alex," she whines.

I press a finger to her needy little button over the rope I tied there. Her body tenses, but she can't move. She's mine.

"I want your dick in me. I need it. Please give it to me."

I pop the button on my jeans to give myself some room. SJ licks her lips. Her eyes track my moves as I lower the zipper. I got a private room for a reason, even if I didn't intend to fuck her, not this first time. But how many more opportunities will I have before she goes home?

"Don't leave me floating here by myself. I want you. Please let me taste." She lets her mouth fall open in invitation.

Does she know what she's asking? Is she serious? "Yellow."

"What?" Her eyes are fully open now.

"Let's slow down a second here, rabbit. Oral's a hard limit for you. What are you doing?"

What am *I* doing? Taking a step back and pausing the scene of my dreams. But she's asking for something that doesn't make sense.

"I feel safe, beautiful, wanted—for me. It feels right to try to let go of the past, with you." Her words grip my heart and tug it out of my chest.

"SJ." There's a story I don't know, but I don't need to right now. In my bag, I find my small red ball. A safe word for when my bunnies can't speak. "Hold this." I wrap her fingers tight around the squishy rubber. "You drop it, we stop. You're still in control, little rabbit." I brush my fingers against her temple and fall into her gaze. She's got me bound up in her more tightly than I have her tied in my ropes.

"I trust you, Alex."

Her words move me. "Okay, little rabbit. We'll try this." I free myself enough to place the head of my cock to her lips. Her tongue peeks out, the tip making the barest contact with my head. A shiver runs up my spine. It's too good.

She opens her mouth. I tilt my hips and—

The door to the room slams open. Stone. A man in a brown uniform rushes in behind him. And another in a blue uniform. Yelling. Chaos.

What the fuck? I step back, tuck my dick away.

"Alexander Craig. You're under arrest."

I freeze. I know that voice, heard it say the exact same words years ago in another place. My guts go watery, and my legs threaten to give out. The sheriff. Alyss's dad. What the hell is he doing here?

SJ is sobbing and incoherent. I need to care for her.

Stone steps between SJ and another man dressed in blue.

"I'm sorry, Alex. I'm so sorry." SJ is weeping.

"No, bunny, this has nothing to do with you. You're okay." I reach for her.

"Don't touch her, you animal." The sheriff lurches for me, but Stone holds an arm out to block him.

"Stop, Uncle," SJ wails.

Uncle? Ice freezes my lungs, threading out to my heart, into my throat. I shake my head and take another step back. I've fallen down the rabbit hole.

Stone is talking to the guy in blue, showing him the consent form. I back against the far wall. I don't understand what's going on, but the echoes of the past, the memories of my life being ruined, are in full color, being played out again.

Cade comes in the room and bypasses everyone to grab my arms. "Breathe, Alex. We'll get this figured out."

"Sarah Jane. Are you okay? I'll get you free of this monster." The sheriff picks up my safety scissors I keep within easy reach.

Sarah Jane. Alyss had a cousin— Bile rises in my throat.

She set this up?

The sheriff is tugging on the rope threaded through her braid. He's going to hurt her. I move to stop him, but Cade forces me back. The sheriff slides the scissors against the back of her head and cuts.

Her braid falls free along with my rope.

I gag. "Get her down first." My hands are shaking when I push Cade toward SJ. "Don't let him cut the ropes and break her."

But the man in the blue uniform cradles her. The red ball bounces to the floor.

Safe word.

I move to my sub to offer comfort, working on autopilot. Cade grabs me. "Stop, Alex. You can't do anything."

This is so wrong. I've failed her. Never should have tied her up.

Why did I think I could make this work? Everything she said was a lie. I turn away, walk to the corner, and tuck myself as tightly as I can into the space. I'm dead inside. This is a million times worse than what happened with Alyss.

Someone rubs my back. Cade? I don't deserve to be comforted.

SJ—no, Sarah Jane—is crying and calling to me.

"Here's a blanket." Stone's voice barely reaches my consciousness. It's good someone is taking care of her.

Someone worthy to see to her care.

Someone who isn't me.

***

SJ

I can't stop crying.

I did this to myself.

If only I could die right now.

"There's a back way out." Stone is with us, still trying to help me. I don't deserve it.

"No. We're going out the way we came in so all those perverts can see what you did to my innocent niece."

Innocent. Right. He doesn't care one wit about me. This is all a show designed to humiliate me. Joke's on him. I couldn't be anymore ashamed of myself than I am right now. Alex's face the moment he realized who I am and what I've done will be etched in my memories forever like a scar. The moment when he turned away and hid in the corner tore my soul in two. Each rope they cut severed any connection I had to one of the nicest, hardworking, most attractive man I've ever known. He cares about people, his friends—he even cared about me. I can't fix this any more than I can weave his ropes back together.

We emerge from the hallway to a room full of people. They're silent. Even the DJ has turned off the music. I imagine the police showing up ruined the party vibe. I shiver and pull the blanket tighter around me. I'm sure I look crazy.

Two servers carry big silver coffee pots from the kitchen, probably ordered to try to distract from the spectacle I've made. Blake scowls at me. Flanking his chair is a man I didn't meet and the woman in red. She may be the licensed professional, but I'm the architect of this disaster.

There is no limit to what I'm capable of fucking up.

"Here's my card." The man, who had been standing next to Blake, speaks to Stone. "Have Alex call me. I've got a friend who's a defense lawyer." There's no doubt he's addressing me too. He confirms what I already know —Alex has people who will care for him. I have my uncle, who will use me again and again. Because his decision to perp-walk me through the crowd shows no concern for my feelings.

It's painfully clear the monster in this situation isn't

Alex. The real monster is the man who used a family connection, compromising photos, the seduction of my writing dream, and a story my cousin didn't corroborate to convince me to be the villain.

Tears blur my vision. I search for Amy in the crowd, desperate for her kindness and caring. She's clutching Tyler's crossed arms. His wide stance and cold gaze confirm that he understands what I did. I betrayed them all, and they hate me—for good reason. They may not have all the details yet, but nothing will redeem me.

My legs weaken, and I stumble. My uncle releases his hold on my shoulder, and I drop to my knees. Amy takes a single step toward me, but Tyler holds her back.

That single step cracks the ice that formed over my heart.

Sharp, icy shards shoot through my chest. I gasp for air.

Oh fuck.

I love Alex.

EIGHTEEN

ALEX

Fuck Stone. All I want to do is get back to my normal routine. Build out the condos, work on the second phase of the resort. Pretend this weekend never. Fucking. Happened.

But here I am, walking into some fancy pants lawyer's office that's gonna cost me every dime I have saved to do nothing, because there's nothing to be done. Sheriff Littlejohn—Alyss's dad, SJ's uncle—has no authority in Colorado. And I ain't never stepping foot in Texas again, no matter how much I miss my momma and my family.

I'm not sure how the sheriff convinced the local authorities to do a wellness check. Doesn't matter. They cooked up a big nothin' burger. I hope they choke on it.

The receptionist shows me to a conference room with oil paintings on the walls and cherry wood furniture. "Would you like a water, Mr. Craig?"

I tell the guy no.

"Mr. Litchfield will be with you momentarily."

Lawyer word, "momentarily." In a minute, shortly, in a sec. Those are words I can afford. I can't afford "momentarily." I should get up and walk out right now.

But the door opens, and a sporty-looking guy in dress slacks and a button-down with the sleeves rolled up walks in. "Mr. Craig?"

I stand up and offer my hand. "Alex."

"Alex, I'm Zach. Simon gave me a brief rundown of what happened this weekend, but I want to hear the story from you."

"I'm not here about what happened this weekend. There's no charges, nothing they can do to me. But my friends, practically family, insisted I talk to you about what happened in Texas ten years ago to see if you can help with that."

He indicates a chair for me to sit. "Okay if I take some notes?"

There's a yellow tablet and a pen on the table I didn't notice before. I shrug. "Sure."

We sit. I take a deep breath. This guy looks like someone I should be catching a ball game with, not telling my darkest secret. But I don't want to go home and admit I chickened out. "Ten years ago, in Texas, I got accused of rape."

Zach doesn't flinch and he doesn't write that down.

"I was eighteen. My girlfriend was three days away from her seventeenth birthday. It was graduation, for me. She still had another year. Her dad caught us in the hay barn. And since he's the sheriff of the town I grew up in, well..."

Zach makes a couple scratches on the pad.

"How long had you been dating?"

"Couple years."

"Having sex the whole time?"

I swallow hard. "No. First time."

"Her mom and dad knew you two were dating?"

"Yep. Been to their house multiple times for Sunday dinner after church. They came to my football games. Alyss was a cheerleader."

"So instead of grounding her, calling your mom and dad, the sheriff arrests you. Any reason why?"

Shit. "I had her tied up."

Zach nods, makes a note. "Tell me about how you had her tied? Around the neck? Spread eagle? Paint me a picture."

"God no. Her arms tied together like in a prayer position, over her head." I press my forearms together and lift them up to show him before quickly dropping them. "And a few lines wrapped about her chest, framing her breasts." My face is hot.

"Suspended or anchored anywhere?"

"No." I didn't have the skills back then. "I'd tied her up lot of times before but with our clothes on. She'd let me practice with her."

"Practice?"

"Hojojutsu. I learned it as part of my jiujitsu studies. Not something they taught at the dojo, except for a few restraints. I guess I was fascinated because we use ropes for all kinds of stuff on the ranch. And learning new knots, quick ties, quick releases. It was cool. So I started researching on the internet, and that led me to Shibari. And...well...yeah." I scrub my hand through my hair.

Zach nods. He asks me a few more questions about the exact date, the county in Texas I lived in. If I have any old friends who are still there. I tell him everything I can.

"When you were caught, did the sheriff arrest you?"

"Yeah." The weight of the handcuffs settles on my wrists as if I'm back there. "My dad had to bail me out."

"Did you see a judge?"

"Not right then. I was supposed to see the traveling judge the following week."

"You didn't?"

"My parents packed me up that night and put me on a bus to my older cousin in St. Louis. He got me a job in construction. Ain't been back since."

"All right. Give me a week or two for research and to get an idea of exactly what we're dealing with here." He goes on to explain his billing process but never offers an ounce of hope.

Like I figured, nothing can be done. But at least I can tell Stone and the rest of them I tried.

I blink back the bright sunlight when I step outside the offices. Felt like years passed by in there or at least hours, like it should be night by now.

"Alex?"

SJ.

The sight of her is like a mule kick to the chest.

The door behind me is closed, but I could retreat back inside.

"Please. Listen. I know you don't owe me a word, but I feel like I owe you."

Nothing she says will matter or make a difference, but I'm not gonna argue. Her hair's been fixed sort of. So short, it makes her blue eyes bigger. I stand there and wait for her to be done with me.

"My real name is Sarah Jane Reading. Alyss Little-john is my cousin." She glances up at me, but I don't react. Figured that part out on my own.

"A few years back, I got into...some trouble. My uncle went to California and saved me. Or at least I thought he did." She crosses her arms. "No, he did. But he also took pictures of the situation I was in. A few months ago, he offered to pay for a writing retreat for me so I could become an author like I'd been dreaming of. It wasn't until after I got here that he told me—blackmailed me— into catching or compromising Alyss's rapist. He told me you took advantage of her—abused her. That the situa- tion broke Alyss and that's why his family left him, to move away from everyone who was making fun of her. He convinced me you ruined her life."

Maybe I did. But I ruined my life too.

"He tried to convince me you were a monster who would try to take advantage of me." She shakes her head. "I don't know what I was thinking. I only wanted those pictures back." Her eyes close. "So dumb. Especially when I got to...know you—"

"Fuck me."

She flinches, and I wish I could take it back. My momma didn't raise me to mean for mean's sake.

"My uncle had me believing a lie. My cousin didn't correct me. But I can do something to correct what I've done. I caved to a man who used family ties to blackmail me. I shouldn't have—" She bites her lip and looks at the ground.

I should feel some kind of way about this apology, but I don't. I don't feel anything.

"I refused to return to Texas with Uncle Littlejohn. I know you, Alex. I know who you are, how honorable you are, deep in my heart. I will do whatever I can to fix this." A tear trails down her cheek. It's a nice touch.

I wait a beat. She doesn't say anything else, so I walk to the SUV and get in. I don't look back as I drive out of the lot.

***

SJ

I'm frozen in the spot he left me in front of the lawyer's office. Alex didn't say anything before he left me standing there. I don't even deserve his anger. I don't deserve an argument. I don't exist in his world any longer. This hollow ache inside me might never go away.

A few more tears fall, but I don't deserve to feel sorry for myself either. Everything that led to this moment, I did. And everything I'm going to do from this moment forward will be to try to fix what I can. Not so he'll give me a second chance. It's clear he won't. If I'm honest, I wouldn't give me one. But I have to try to make things right for Alex. He's a good man, and what I did to him was wrong. My family and I... Our jagged edges cut him deep.

With a deep breath, I swallow what's left of my pride and enter the lawyer's office. The guy at the front asks me if I have an appointment. "No, but I have information that could help Mr. Litchfield with Alex Craig's case."

"I'll see if he can make time to see you." The man indicates two empty chairs flanking a window. "Have a seat."

As in "get comfortable, this could be awhile." Half an hour later, I'm shown to a conference room. A man who looks to be in his forties with blond-streaked hair strides in and introduces himself as Zach Litchfield. "Call me Zach."

I explain what I want to do, but he doesn't smile or get excited like I expected.

"Does Alex know you're here?"

"I saw him outside." Maybe not the explanation I should give, but it's true.

"There are no charges pending as a result of your interaction with Mr. Craig. So I'm not sure what your statement can add." As in I'm a waste of his time. It would sting if it were true. But I still believe I can do something to make the situation better.

"I can vouch for his respect for women, the consensual way he dealt with everything between us, and explain what my uncle was up to by blackmailing me."

"Your uncle was blackmailing you?"

"Yes."

"How?"

I turn my head and stare at an oil painting of some mountains, probably somewhere in Colorado. It's a beautiful picture. Not like the one I'm about to paint. "All my life, I wanted to be a model or an actress."

Zach doesn't move.

"I was twenty-one when I got my big break." A bitter laugh pops out of me. "Paid one-way trip to California for a photo shoot. I quit my job and went with a stranger who lied to me. My momma told me not to, but it was one more warning in a long line of them I'd ignored since I was a teenager. Turned out she was right. It wasn't—well, it was a photo shoot, but not for clothes or anything. In fact, the first instruction was to take all my clothes off." My throat closes at the memories.

Zach slides over a box of tissues and a bottle of water. I didn't realize I was crying. After a few minutes of trying to compose myself, I suck in a deep breath. I'm not the victim here. Alex is.

"My uncle, the man who was married to my aunt while I was growing up, came to California and rescued me before things got worse. Worse than they already were. My momma must have called him. I'm not sure. I returned home, went to community college for graphic design and marketing. Getting my life together sort of. Until my uncle came to town a few months ago and offered a paid trip to Colorado. Said he wanted to help me get my life on track, being as we're family and all. It wasn't until I was already here that he threatened to post pictures he had from California. I didn't even know he had them." I gag at the recall of my mouth around the dick of a stranger I was forced to blow. "Told me he'd show my momma, my boss, he'd post them on the internet. Unless I did this one thing for him."

"What's that?"

"Help him take down Alex." I didn't have any idea I could be more ashamed of myself than I was in California. Turns out I can be.

"What do you know about what happened when he was dating your cousin?"

I repeat the question in my head, not quite following the change of topic. "I know she stopped spending summers with me once they started dating."

"But you didn't see them together?"

"Maybe once or twice at Thanksgiving or Christmas. But it was holiday time, so I think I met him briefly, maybe? She was gaga over him. Would post pictures about all the stuff they did together and send me emails." Oh wow. I'd forgotten about that. All the messages we sent each other with our thoughts and dreams, like a shared diary. Like any teenager, I didn't pay that much attention to what she said, I was so wrapped up in my own dreams of fame.

"Do you have access to those?"

"No, she took down all her social media after her junior year. Quit sending me emails too. Then my uncle and aunt got divorced and Alyss and my aunt moved to Charleston. I haven't seen them in person since then."

She shut down, and I didn't even notice. Went on with my life like she didn't matter. I owe her an apology too.

"Do you have the emails she sent you?"

"Yeah. I'm terrible about deleting stuff."

"Good." He slides a tablet and a pen over to me. "Write down everything you just told me and everything you remember about that time when Alyss and Alex were dating. Then, if you're willing, I'd like you to log into your email and we can print those old messages."

"Will this help Alex?"

"It might."

A tiny spark of hope flares to life in my empty core.

It's late afternoon before I finish. I forgot how chatty Alyss was about Alex. It was the ramblings of teenage girls, one with her first love. Or at least her first crush. But maybe it will help him. I'm wrung out like a wet rag by the time I leave Zach's office. And I still have to pick up my stuff from the Sunflower before I leave town. I dread facing Amy and Tyler and especially Stone.

I call before I leave the parking lot.

"Thank you for calling Sunflower Inn."

"Amy?"

She sucks in a breath.

"Would it be okay if I came to get my things?"

"When?" That answer stings, but what do I expect?

"Now. I'm about twenty-five minutes away."

"Sure. I was wondering what I was supposed to do with—"

She stops midsentence. Wondering what to do with my shit.

"Thank you for not throwing it out. I stayed at a hotel near the airport. Figured it'd be better if I kept my distance."

She doesn't say anything.

"Okay. See you soon." I end the call, hollowed out and now run over. I don't think I could feel any lower. At least I hope not.

At the door of the Sunflower, I pause, unsure if I should knock or what. The door opens, and a somber Amy is clinging to the other side. "Thanks for letting me in."

She nods. "Your room is as you left it. Let me know if you need anything."

Your friendship. Alex's love. A place to belong. "Thank you."

The climb up the stairs is like revisiting an old memory, except Alex won't be waiting up there. I won't be tucked away, writing my book, surrounded by friendship and love I'd barely become a part of before I burned it all down. With everything shoved in my two bags and my laptop in my carryon satchel, there's nothing left of me here. The beautiful room is unscathed from my heartless actions, unlike Alex. Unlike his friends. Unlike me.

As if I'm worthy of feeling sorry for myself.

I wrestle my bags down the stairs as quietly as I can, but Amy is waiting at the check-in desk, the same way she was when I arrived those months ago. One difference —no welcoming smile.

"Thank you." I wait for her to respond, but she doesn't. "I'm sorry for everything."

"Safe travels, SJ."

As goodbyes go, it's probably kinder than I deserve. But the chilly dismissal makes it obvious I've ruined my relationship with the best people I've ever known.

The drive to the airport takes forever. I don't have a ticket booked, but there's a flight leaving in forty-five minutes for Dallas. Gives me barely enough time to make it across the huge airport and through security. I haven't eaten since the free hotel breakfast this morning, but I'm not hungry. I'm not anything.

When I finally make it back to my apartment after midnight, it doesn't feel like home. Everything is where I left it but coated in a layer of dust and detachment. I check my mailbox, stuffed with late bills and final notices. Nothing I can do about them right now. My savings will be enough to catch up the bills. I'll pay my landlord the month I owe him too. Until I get another real job, I can make do with internet gigs. They don't pay well, but it'll be enough. It's not like I need much.

Except answers. When I remembered all those emails Alyss sent, it's odd that she couldn't even talk about Alex. I know he didn't rape her. Deep in my heart, that's not the man he is, and I can't believe that's the man he was. There's nothing holding me here, not even a half-dead houseplant. But there is something demanding my attention right now. The truth.

I plug in my laptop and book a flight to Charleston. Alyss will have to be honest if I confront her in person. I won't accept anything less.

NINETEEN

ALEX

"Brother, did you sleep here?"

I lean back on my heels and stare up at Gabe. "We're racing time, bro. Gotta finish this phase before the snows hit and we can't get any subs out here."

"We're ahead of schedule on the second phase of condos, and I thought you had a team coming to do the tiling."

Tile sucks. I hate working on my knees and cutting and recutting each piece until it fits perfectly. But it's better than hanging around the Sunflower waiting for Sarah Jane to reappear. Waiting for my heart to start beating again. Waiting to give a shit about anything. "Figured I could make some progress before they show up. Should be here in an hour."

He frowns at me. "Alright. I'm gonna check the fixtures in 301 and 302. Painters should be here soon. And Delilah said she might drop by."

I groan. I've been avoiding anyone and everyone who was at the soft opening. Everyone who witnessed my complete failure. Especially her. Maybe I can take lunch when she shows up and let Gabe deal with her. Again.

I drop to my knees and focus on the tile. At least there's something I'm good at. Might as well hang up my ropes forever. Or I would if they weren't long gone to the landfill. I still have a few lengths in my closet. When we move out of the Sunflower, I'll toss them too. Everyone still thinks I'm staying here, living at the resort, but I figure I'm better off heading back to my cousin in St. Louis. Or maybe I'll head up to Montana or down to Florida. Nothing tying me to any of these places except people who pity me. At least in a new place, I can start over. No clubs. No women. No risk. Can't lose everything if you give it away.

It's well after dark when I let myself into the Sunflower that night. There's a single light on in the kitchen. Amy probably saved me a plate. I leave my tool bag on the first stair to take up after I eat. The small bath has a fancy towel, so I shake off my hands good enough and grab a paper towel before I shove my plate in the microwave for three minutes like Amy's note said to do. She's like a mom, taping notes to plates of food in the fridge. My momma used to do that for me when we did two-a-days for football. I love that she cares, and I hate that I disappointed her. Both of them. I take my plate and my drink to the dining room, not bothering with a light. But as soon as I sit down, the overhead flips on.

Stone.

I close my eyes before I tilt my head to the ceiling. No avoiding the conversation any longer. The chair across from me shifts against the flooring. I open my eyes to face Stone sitting across from me. Rather than give in and talk, I shove a bite of casserole in my mouth. *Fuck.* It's hot. I open my mouth around my food and huff air in and out in an attempt to cool it. Kind of rude, but so is waiting in the dark to ambush me.

Finally, I'm able to chew and swallow. I take a gulp of milk.

"Working late again."

I nod and blow on my next bite of dinner.

"Delilah says you're ahead of schedule. Having to rearrange the subs to get them in earlier."

"Weather could shift at any time. Mountains are unpredictable." I shove the forkful in and chew carefully.

"I heard every word that night, including 'Yellow.' You have no reason to second-guess yourself."

I swallow. Put my fork on the plate. "Whatever you need to say, say it. Because this is the last time I'm talking about it."

"You did everything right. If I thought for one second you were fucking up, I'd have stopped the action myself."

"Why'd you let the cops in, then?" The question has been at the back of my mind for days as I twist and turn the events over and over, trying to figure out how it went so wrong.

"Elliot sent them downstairs to avoid a scene above. They were demanding a welfare check. We can't afford to get sideways with the locals before we open. So I let it play out, figuring SJ would give a thumbs-up and it would be over. I didn't know her uncle was involved." Stone swipes a hand over his face. "I had no reservations about opening the door because everything was consensual. You're an excellent Dom."

"Not a Dom. A top."

"Everything you did that night was perfect. The precautions you took were exactly right. Nothing that went wrong was your fault or failure."

Sure the fuck feels like it. But what the fuck would Stone know about being inadequate? Fucker is made of granite and authority. I'm just some Podunk cowboy with a fucking lasso and a fixation on Japanese culture. Too bad I don't like sushi. Would have been so much simpler than my passion for tying women up.

"Same is true for what happened in Texas."

How the fuck does he know what happened in Texas? I'm about to ask him, but he cuts me off.

"You had Dom drop, and you haven't recovered from it."

"What are you talking about?" Might have been true at the time when I was in the scene with SJ, but that's been...two weeks and three days. I'm over it. Soon I'll be over her. Any day now.

"Dom drop. Like sub drop. But at this point, a blanket, some chocolate, and a cuddle ain't gonna fix it."

"Well thank fuck for small favors, because I'm not sure I could handle you trying to cuddle me, Stone. Doing the dad, sneak-up conversation is about all I can take."

"I'll hug you if you need a damn hug. But that won't fix this. You need to scene again."

"No. I don't." Not now. Not ever. Done with that.

"You're doing a demonstration. Grand opening. Get your shit figured out. Tyler ordered some ropes for you. Should be here in the next few days. Plenty of time for you to prep them and think about what you want to do."

What I want to do is *not* give a demonstration. "Don't have a partner."

"Cassie said she'd do it."

"Cassie, the bartender?"

"There a problem?"

Did he growl at me? Also, he's puffed up and there's murder in his eyes. This man knows five ways to kill me at this table with no additional tools. Not sure how I forgot that for the moment. "No problem at all. Figured she would be working."

"We have plenty of backup. You're doing the scene."

"Fine."

Stone goes upstairs, leaving me to wonder when he talked to Cassie and Tyler. And who else was in on this plan? And what the fuck I'm going to do with a sub I can't touch? Because I'm certain if I touch her in any kind of sexual way—not that I would—Stone will come unhinged and no one will ever find my body. Even if *he* doesn't realize it, I have no doubt.

SJ

The flight to Charleston was too easy. And the rideshare had no problem finding their way to my cousin's house. Hard to miss the multistory white historical mansion with black shutters blocks from the Ashley River. My cousin has done well for herself. I grab my roller case from the sidewalk and heft it up ten brick stairs to the enamel black door with a brass pineapple knocker. I texted her I would be in the city for work, so she's expecting me, but I still hesitate. She has a husband, kids, and I'm carrying past troubles to her doorstep.

It's for Alex. And for her. I went on with my life when hers fell apart like she didn't even matter. I owe her an apology. I lift the knocker and rap twice. The wrought iron fencing holds my attention as I wait for someone to answer. It's simple but elegant. Understated and probably expensive. The door, at least eight feet tall, opens soundlessly, and my beautiful blonde cousin, not touched by the years that have passed or the kids she's had, is standing inside a tall narrow hallway inviting me in. I wipe my feet as if I can scrape off the dirt I'm bringing with me.

I leave my bag in the entry to the side of the door and follow her into the all-white kitchen with stainless steel appliances.

"It's so good to see you, Sarah Jane. How was your flight?"

I let her make small talk while she puts two glasses of iced tea on a tray along with a plate of cookies.

"Where are the kids?" It would be nice to meet my...

not nephews. Cousins, with some kind of math attached like second and removed.

"Preschool and the sitter. I didn't want to miss a moment to catch up. How many days are you here for?"

"Two. I head back Friday night." Wednesday is the cheapest day to fly out, and I can't afford the hotel until Monday, so it was a compromise.

"You should stay with us. If it's not too far from where you're working."

"I don't want to be an inconvenience." Or for her to realize I lied about coming out for work.

She laughs. "It's no bother. We have bedrooms to spare."

"The company paid for the room. But thank you. It's so great to see you again. It's been so long. Time flies and all that." Why am I awkward around the person who used to be my favorite family member? Because we have to have a hard conversation.

We sit at a small round glass table in two of the four white cane chairs with padded seats. The windows in the round room make it feel like we're outside, sitting under the green-leafed trees. "Your home is beautiful."

"It's been in Charles's family forever. I'd rather be on the Isle of Palms in a modern build—less upkeep, bigger rooms, closer to the beach—but he loves this old place." There's fondness in her tone.

"Are you happy? Is he good to you?" I suddenly have to know that she's okay.

"He's my best friend, and yes, he's very good to me. Even indulges my occasional wildness. We met when I started at the high school here. It wasn't easy transitioning my entire life as a senior. No friends. No cheerleading team. No familiarity at all."

"I can't imagine. Why'd your mom make such a big move then? Wouldn't it have been better to wait one more year?" I'm pushing and she might toss me out, but I have to know the truth, if she'll tell me. If she can be honest with herself.

She sips her tea. I break one of the cookies in half and take a bite. The buttery dough melts in my mouth, pecans tasting like home.

"I've thought about that time a lot since you called. It was the worst moment of my life."

"Because Alex hurt you?"

"No. Not at all." She shakes her head, and a slight smile lifts the corners of her mouth. "We'd waited so long. I had to beg him because I knew he would be busy on the ranch. Might even have enrolled in tech school or something. I would be stuck in town, finishing my senior year. I wanted that connection to him."

"What happened?" Please don't say he took advantage of you. I can't believe that about him.

"My father caught us. Arrested Alex. Grounded me for life." She shakes her head.

"What about him tying you?"

She gapes at me. "You know about that?"

I nod, not sure how much to say.

"I blocked out that time in my life so hard, left it all behind. I have a new life that I love. But it's a life that depends on appearance and duty in some ways. I'm the wife of a prominent doctor, from a prominent family, in a social circle I wasn't born to. I've had to learn how to fit in. And I wanted to. There's nothing about my life I would change except for what my dad did all those years ago. But if he hadn't, I wouldn't have met Charles. He's truly my person."

I understand what she means. Alex could have been my person. Would have been under different circumstances. But circumstances are all we have to work with. "I owe you an apology. I wasn't there for you the way I should have been. Didn't even reach out when your parents split."

"Please don't be sorry." She rests her hand on my forearm briefly. "I could have called you too. Even if you had, I'm not sure what I would have said. It was overwhelming at the time, with Alex gone, moving here. I'm not sure what you could have said or done about any of it."

"I don't want to upset your apple cart, but your daddy went after Alex. And he used me to do it."

"Oh God. Sarah Jane, did my father get violent with you?"

"No." But the fact violence is her first thought tells me why her momma left the asshole. "He used compromising pictures of me." I give her the world's shortest version of the tale of my greatest shame. Well, second greatest now.

"That man is the devil. I hate that he's my father. I look for signs of him in my kids in case it's genetic. But they're both little gentlemen, like their daddy." Alyss smiles and her gaze softens. She's happy.

"I fell in love with Alex."

"What?" A carbon copy of my own blue eyes laser in on me.

"In Colorado, I was living out there in an inn where Alex lives, and I got to know him." I bite my lip while searching for the right word. "Intimately."

"Oh my. Has he changed much since you knew him back in high school?"

"I didn't remember him. I only met him a couple of times, and he was yours, so I didn't pay that close attention." I hesitate, but I can't help but tell her how great he is. "He works in construction. He's talented, both with building and managing others. He's a total gentleman too."

"Does he... Is he still into martial arts?" She's focused on the table, can't meet my eyes. It's clear what she's asking.

"He's still into ropes."

Her cheeks turn red.

"There's nothing wrong with that, as long as it's consensual." There. I've opened the door for her.

"No. There's not." Her voice is barely above a whisper. "I tried to explain that to my father. Tried to talk him out of arresting Alex. Tried to talk him into dropping the charges, that everything Alex did, I asked for." She cups her cheek, gaze still unfocused. "My dad hit me. Called me a slut and a liar." She lifts her chin, her gaze pointed and fierce. "That's when my momma left him and took me with her."

Hate for M.D. Littlejohn churns in my gut. What a complete bastard. "He was wrong."

"I broke up their marriage. It wasn't perfect, but it wasn't violent. Not until that night."

"That you know of."

She waves her hand to dispel my argument. "My family was steady until that night—maybe not the picture of love, but solid. Alex was gone before I got to say good-bye. We left a day later. I put that part of my life in the past and moved on. Otherwise, I would have lost my mind."

"Did you love Alex?"

"As much as a teen girl could, I suppose. We were like chess pieces on a board. Meant to be together, football king and perky cheerleader. We might have married. Had some kids and our own kind of solid, steady life. Easy. Like a thousand other stories."

Does she have any idea how spectacular that kind of life sounds to me? A little house on some land, a man I love, and kids who are happy. Does she have any idea that despite it being a thousand stories—an ordinary miracle—it's still a miracle when it happens? "You were always meant for more. Always shined a little too bright for that town."

She nods like I see her. And I do.

"I love my life here. I love what I've become and how I've found my place in such a rare community. People here wouldn't understand what I was doing with Alex.

I'm not even sure I do." She laughs, but it sounds like the laugh in a play, rehearsed and only for effect.

I check my watch. "I have dinner with a client tonight, so I have to get checked into my hotel."

"Oh no. I was hoping you could stay for dinner and meet Charles and the kids." It's a sweet lie. But I'm part of her past she's still trying to erase. I can't blame her. I'd gladly take my own eraser to my past if that was possible.

"I would love to meet them if I can before I leave. I'm sorry this is such a rushed trip, but I'm glad I got to see you. One thing... Your dad is still going after Alex, but there is a lawyer trying to help him. I told him my story. If you want to help, for old times' sake, put a wrong to right, I'll leave you his card." I hand her the tiny rectangle that could change Alex's world. "I'm happy for you and the life you've created. A life that fits you."

She walks me out. There's still a shred of hope in me that my cousin will do the right thing. She's a good person, doing the best she can to build her life too.

Back at the hotel, I stare at my laptop, reread the words I've written in my book, and try to draft a happily ever after. It's a required ending, but I'm having trouble imagining one. I close the lid and pull out the rope bundle Alex gave me for practice before he hated me. The ropes pressing into my skin is the only way I can connect to him, the only way I feel grounded and like I might have a future.

I spend the next day checking out a plantation and walking on the beach. No point in coming all the way out here and not seeing some stuff. The plantation is off-putting. A history of a culture I struggle to relate to and the ruins of a past that can't be healed. The beach speaks to me. The waves wash on the shore like a heartbeat. Not like they crashed against the land in California, the one time I saw it. This ocean is soft in its strength—no need to scream it. I hope my cousin will find her inner strength and help Alex. I hope I'm able to find mine and figure out how to live without him. Someday.

TWENTY

ALEX

My phone rings and I answer without looking, one hand still holding the screwdriver I need to put on the light switch cover. Detail work, but someone has to do it.

"Alex. Zach Litchfield. Good news."

What's a lawyer's definition of good news? He sent me a bill? "Hey, Zach."

"All past charges in Texas have been dropped. Can't be brought again."

The screwdriver slips from my fingers and lands on the bedroom carpet. The switch plate hangs in place, held on by nothing. Like me in this moment. There's a small lip of reality that my mind is clinging to because I can't have heard him right. "How? Why?"

"Besides the statute of limitations issue, there was the notarized statement from Sarah Jane. And it seems Alyss Littlejohn Hayward sent a letter directly to the judge explaining her side of the tale."

I drop to my ass, my legs no longer working. "Alyss? Sent a letter?" She left town shortly after I did. Didn't stay to finish high school in town. "Why would she do that?"

"I have a copy of the letter if you want to read it, but it mentions her cousin came for a visit and her father's current actions against you couldn't remain unchecked."

SJ spoke to Alyss. And now I'm free. No sword hanging over my head. Doesn't change anything, and yet, it changes everything. "I can see my family?"

"You can do whatever you want."

"Thank you."

"You're welcome. My assistant will mail you a final statement at the end of the month. And if you see SJ, let her know the pictures won't be a problem in the future."

I mouth some kind of answer, and the call is over and my life is my own for the first time. First, I finish fixing the plate to the wall. After that, I call the airlines. Gabe is in the condo next door on the second floor, checking the bathroom plumbing for leaks. He pops out from under the sink when I call his name.

"What's up?"

"I have to go."

"Grabbing lunch?"

I check my watch. It is that time, but I'm too antsy to eat. "No, a flight back home. Gotta pack. Be back in a week."

He stands up with a hop to get his prosthetic leg under him, wipes his hands on his jeans. "Everything okay?"

"It's good. Everything's good. But I haven't seen my family in ten years, and I need to go."

"Alright then, brother." He grabs my hand. "Safe journey. I'll be here when you get back."

I give him a half hug and pat on the back, grab my tool bag, and head for the Sunflower.

Stone offers to drive me to the airport, but I decide to leave my truck in long-term parking. I'm cutting the time to get on the plane close with the drive to Denver International, and it's late when I land in Dallas. Luckily, I'm able to rent a car. It's a tiny thing I have to fold in half to fit into, but I'd shape myself into an origami swan and fly home if I had to at this point.

A long drive later, I realize my family is probably already in bed. Day starts early on the ranch, but I couldn't wait another minute to see them. The porch light is on, its orange glow so familiar and welcoming. How many nights did I return home to this view, without appreciating the wide plank porch, the swing, even the blooming pots of geraniums my momma puts out in the summer? Home. It calls to me, invites me to walk up the two steps, and hesitate about what to do next. Never have knocked on my own front door before. I know my home, but I'm not completely sure of my place here anymore.

I clench my jaw, roll my fingers into a fist, and rap on the door. Three quick bursts. I half expect to hear a shotgun being prepped to pepper whoever the asshole is on my daddy's front porch. Instead, his face appears in the opening, blinking away the sleep.

Concern melts away replaced by shock. "Alex?"

"Hi, Daddy."

The door flies open, and my father tugs me across the entry and into his arms. This is no man hug. This is a long-lost son being embraced, enfolded back into everything he's lost. My eyes sting. He calls to my mom over my shoulder. Footsteps flying down the stairs prompts him to release me. A tear tracks down his cheek.

"Oh." My momma's gasp pulls my heart from my chest. She's on the bottom step, hand on her heart.

"I'm here, Momma."

"My boy," she says, launching off the stairs and wrapping herself around me.

I don't remember her being so tiny. She's a force larger than life that whooped me more than once when I deserved it. But somehow, the ten years have stripped away her fierceness. Left her a little colorless and soft. But she smells the same, and her tears can still shred my heart.

"You're here." She leans back and holds my cheeks. Water fills her blue-gray eyes. "You're finally here."

"Sorry to be so late." I say it like I missed curfew, not that I missed a decade. Seeing my family over internet video chats on the rare occasion they could get a good enough connection to sustain a call is nothing close to standing in my home with my parents. Seeing everything is the same as when I left. This is what I lost. This is what I missed. This is what I came home for.

She sniffs. "You must be hungry. Let me fix you something. Your room is waiting for you."

I eat everything she puts on my plate. Cold ham.

Reheated mashed potatoes and gravy. A scoop of green beans and a couple cold corn fritters I dip in maple syrup. Her homemade biscuit is on the edge of being dry, but I slap some butter on it and savor every crumb. My parents sit at the kitchen table with me, silently watching. Probably a lot like how they looked at me as a newborn. Theirs, but unfamiliar. Eating, so that's a good thing.

The cold glass of milk is the perfect finish. I set down the glass, and exhaustion hits me. I worked so hard to get here, and now that I am, all I want to do is sleep in my own room, in my own bed. "Want some help with the cows in the morning?"

My dad nods, a hint of a smile on his lips.

"Best get to bed, then. I hear they don't sleep in like they used to." It's an old joke. How I was teaching the animals to sleep in so they could get more rest when I didn't get up on time.

"I've been slacking on their training." He stands, and my mom takes my plate. I offer to wash it, but she waves me away.

I kiss her cheek before I head up the stairs, taking my bag from the entryway with me. My room is exactly as I left it. No dust. Ribbons and trophies on a shelf mounted to the wall. Posters that have yellowed and curled. My black belt hangs in the closet with my gi. A picture of Alyss and me at junior prom. We look like babies. I put it facedown, not sure how my momma dealt with looking at it constantly when she cleaned the room. But nothing that happened was Alyss's fault. I'm too tired to figure out my feelings except quiet joy at being home. I strip down and crawl between the sheets on a bed that's slightly too short now. A couple punches to my pillow, and I'm out.

Despite the fact I'm still on Colorado time, I'm up and ready to spend the day working. Not that different than my normal day, except that I'm home. Momma has breakfast on the table when I come downstairs. Some things have changed. New curtains in the windows, and Daddy invested in some automation and has a couple of hired hands to help. He'll need it if he wins the election for sheriff. Still can't believe he's running, but the county is tired of M.D. Littlejohn and his dictator bullshit.

The ranch isn't quite as big as I remembered it. None of the horses I rode are still here, but I still remember how to ride, even if I am sore the first couple of days. I help with construction projects, fixing the fence, and patching a tiny leak in the barn. At night, I tell them stories about my life in Colorado. About how Blake is healing and the resort property is coming along. They tell me the latest gossip since the last time we had a call, which was longer ago than I remembered. I fit here and I'm family, but I'm still a visitor. Despite being in the places where Alyss and I spent so many hours, it's not her I miss. SJ crosses my mind more times than I care to admit. Things I want to tell her about my day, places I want to show her. She hurt me, flayed my heart, but she's the one whose absence I feel there now.

My heart is a dumbass.

Sunday, after church, all the neighbors gather for the barbecue my parents are putting on in honor of my visit.

Everyone—from my old football coach to my once best friend's parents—is there. Neighbors in a ten-mile radius have brought their offering to the meal. The tables groan under corn casseroles, cornbread, potato salad, macaroni salad, bean salad, baked beans, pinto beans, and more kinds of pie than I can identify. Daddy has two full briskets, racks of ribs, and burgers and hot dogs for the kids. I haven't seen a crowd this big since the last football game I played in. But then they were seated in the stands. Now, I'm visiting with everyone and telling the story of where I am and what I'm doing over and over again. A few ask if I'm married yet or have a girlfriend. But only a few. Most know why I left town. I'm sure some of them still believe I'm guilty. Truth can be harder to find than a sober man at a bar. And it rarely tells a better story than a drunken lie.

As the party winds to a close and folks fill up their trucks and minivans with their families, a familiar and unwelcome sight rolls up the road to our driveway. Lights flashing, the sheriff's car skids to a stop and M.D. Littlejohn slides out of the driver's side, placing his hat on his balding but still crew-cut head. He hitches up the waistband on his pants and strides over to my father at the head of the drive. Several of the ranchers join him, along with a couple well-known citizens, like the chief of the volunteer fire fighters and our banker, Mr. Curtis.

"What can I do for ya, M. D.?" I note my daddy doesn't use the sheriff's title for the first time in my hearing.

"Heard your boy was in my county."

I move to stand next to my father and cross my arms. "What can I do you for?"

"Got a warrant for your arrest." He lifts the cuffs off his utility belt and slaps them in his palm.

My guts liquify for a hot second before shifting to ice. Not. Again. "Got a piece of paper proving that?"

"Everyone here knows what you did to my daughter, Alex Craig." He pitches his voice loud enough that anyone in this county or the next could hear him.

"You mean, Alyss? The one who's living in Charleston with her husband the doctor who wrote a letter to the judge who dismissed your trumped-up charges? That daughter?"

He gapes like a catfish cleaning the bottom of a pond. Did he assume I wouldn't know?

"Unless you have a piece of paper, signed by the judge, I'm not going anywhere with you. I'm not some green teenage boy caught with his pants down, Sheriff. Not this time." If he's going to call me out, I might as well finish painting the picture.

"Do they know you had to tie her up? That you can't be with a woman unless you restrain her because no sane woman would want you? Pervert."

"Well, Sheriff." I tilt my hat back and scratch my hair before replacing it. "Being that gossip travels through this town like a twister on rails, I'm pretty sure they already know. But if by chance some of them missed it, now they do. And no, I'm not embarrassed by my love of ropes and all things ranching or my fascination with the Japanese artform of Shibari. As you well know. And being that these folks all came out here for Sunday dinner, to celebrate my homecoming with my family, I'd say most of them don't care." My mother is standing at my side. "They probably do still wonder why your wife left you so abruptly. And they'll wonder later why you tried to arrest me on charges the judge already tossed out. Might even make them nervous to vote for you in the next election once they figure out you don't follow the law."

"I am the law."

"No sir. You aren't. You're an angry little man who has made my life and that of my family's miserable for far too long. Now unless you have a piece of paper you want to show me, I'll say, 'Good day, sir.'" If he pulls out a warrant, I'll die right here. He goes to his car, opens the door, and leans in.

Fuck, he's calling my bluff.

He pulls off his hat and places it on the passenger seat.

Is he leaving?

He stands back up and points his finger at me. "This ain't over. One day, you'll get what's coming to you."

"I'm sure the Lord will provide for you as well," I respond.

———

A FEW DAYS LATER, I'm carrying my suitcase down the stairs.

"You sure you can't stay a while longer, son?" My daddy's question stings because I hate disappointing him and I've loved being here. My mother, clinging to his arm and blinking up at me, doesn't help.

"I didn't give them much notice when I left. Promised I'd be back to finish the resort in time for the grand opening. And since I've got a stake in it..." My shoulders rise as the finish of my explanation.

"Proud of you, son. Despite everything, you're doing something with your life. Literally building something." He claps my shoulder. "Proud of you."

Someday we'll have to have a discussion about the ranch, but not for several more years. Who knows. I might want to settle down here again. Or maybe the suburbs will have pushed so far out, the ranch will be a gated community. My parents will retire and finally see some of the world. I don't know, but now I can return anytime they need me.

"You'll be here for Christmas, right?" Momma grips my forearm in her still strong hand. "Your sister's coming with Ray and the kids."

"Promise. Nothing could keep me away." Except maybe one of those damn Texas ice storms. Hell, I'd rent a sled and get my ass here if I had to, because I'm not disappointing them again. Ever.

When I finally get back to the Sunflower that night, the place is dark, but the front light turns on automatically when it detects my movement. One of the upgrades Blake and his team did before his accident. My key slides easily in the lock, and I drag myself in. The trip back seemed to take twice as long as the trip to Dallas. A faint hint of lemon oil lingers in the air. There's a single light on in the living room area.

"Stone." I acknowledge the silent man in the chair.

"Alex. How's the family?"

"Good. It was a good trip."

"Any trouble with that Mad Dog sheriff?"

Not sure how Stone knows the sheriff's nickname, but it's Stone. "Nothing I couldn't handle."

"Glad you're back. The final inspection is scheduled for next week. Gabe's done an excellent job of filling in, but I'd like your eyes on it. We've got some buyers ready to close, and Amy's almost ready to put this place on the market. All depends on being able to move in."

"Sure, it won't be a problem." I have my one-bedroom unit waiting for me. Living on site will make the next phases much easier. No commute. Guess I've committed to staying. Wasn't completely sure until this moment. But as much as I love my family, I have a future here. One I've worked hard for. Earned all on my own.

"You'll be ready to do the demonstration at the Grand Opening of the club."

It's a statement, not a question, but I respond anyway. "I'm good. No problem."

"Glad to hear it." He stands up and turns off the light. "If you find someone else to do the demo with, let me or Cassie know."

I'm in the dark until he flips the switch at the bottom of the stairway. He's halfway up before I get my bag and follow.

"See you in the morning," he says over his shoulder before disappearing around the bend.

I'm quiet as I head to the opposite end of the hall. There's a pang of loss that lingers as I pass SJ's room, but that will fade with time, like those posters on my childhood bedroom walls that I took down and threw away before I left Texas. It's okay to let things go, even if they once meant something to you. But people aren't posters, and it might take me a lot longer to get over the redhead who lassoed my heart before leaving it shredded under her heel.

TWENTY-ONE

SJ

I'm working on a graphics gig for a fantasy author when the email comes in. *Grand opening of the Yacht Club.* They must not have scrubbed the list before the notice went out, because I'm sure they didn't intend to invite me. But now that I've seen the invite, I want nothing more than to be there.

I close the message and get back to work. Freelancing has been a greater success than I expected. I'm getting more word-of-mouth recommendations. Enough to pay my bills and put a little bit back into savings. Enough that I haven't looked for another corporate job. Enough to keep my mind off Alex during the day.

The nights are a different story. I dream of walking down the hallway in the Sunflower and finding him with his hand around his cock, stroking its length and calling my name. I dream of him tying me up and fucking me senseless. Some nights are ugly, and I dream of falling and him not being there to catch me. Or worse, watching as I drop. I still practice with my one length of rope. Watch all the videos on self-tying I can find. I've even priced out one of the tripod suspension devices that can be setup in a living room. They aren't cheap, but it is tempting.

Maybe I'll spring for it if I ever finish my book. I fiddle with the sentences, tweak the tension, up the sensual scenes, but I can't write the ending. I joined a writer's group online and asked for advice. One of them responded requesting details about the grand gesture. I don't think my book has one. Unless a silent standoff could be considered a gesture. It's more like flipping the bird at each other. If I were writing a Western, this would be when the whistling music would play and the bullets would fly. Pretty sure that ending would kill any chance of marketing my book as a romance.

I finish the graphics job and submit it a couple hours later. Unable to resist, I open the invite again. It's good. I could have designed something a little better, but it's not bad. Has all the pertinent info, which is a win and low bar that is missed more often than not. I continue to study it as an idea takes shape. A terrible idea. A totally bad plan. I'll need help to pull it off. Amy would tell Tyler, so it can't be her. Stone scares me too much to approach with my horrible plan.

I scroll through my contacts. Katherine.

I stare at the number, not ready to dial it. I put my phone down and check for more gigs.

It takes me two more days to find the courage to call.

"Hello?" Katherine sounds wary when she answers.

"Hey, Katherine. It's SJ, Sarah Jane." Hopefully she doesn't hang up.

"It's been a while. How are you?" There's a hint of frost in her tone. I deserve it.

"Getting by. I'm calling because I got an invitation the grand opening." My stomach knots, waiting for her to tell me it was a mistake.

"Are you planning to attend?"

"Maybe." I shrug as if she can see me. "I assume you are. Gabe has worked so hard on the construction. And I checked out the website. It's stunning."

"You gave me some great copy to work with. And of course we won't miss it. At least the first part."

"I saw there's supposed to be a rope demonstration."

"Alex. Not sure how he'll have the energy. He and Gabe have put so many hours into making sure everything is perfect, organizing the subs and inspections. But it's all coming together. Thought I'd lose my mind when Alex went home for a week."

Alex was in Texas?

"I barely saw Gabe, and we had preteen twin boys staying with us."

I don't know how they manage being foster parents. I can't take care of a houseplant at this point. But Katherine is older than me. And Gabe was in the military, so he probably learned to run a tight ship.

"Do you still have the boys?" Maybe that's why they aren't staying.

"No, moved on to family members. That's usually

better for the kids. So if you're coming out, we have plenty of room if you need a place to stay."

Maybe that wasn't frost. Maybe it's Katherine's New York accent coming through.

"I assume you're coming out here to make a big apology?"

Ouch. But she's not wrong. "I have to try. I miss him so much." I miss all of them.

"For what it's worth, I think Alex misses you, too."

My heart pounds in my chest with longing and hope. "I probably should have tried to call him."

"Some things are best done in person. You know, I absolutely believe in redemption. People make mistakes, especially if they're listening to family. My father's influence led me to make a lot of bad decisions. But when you're in the wrong, you have to apologize as big or bigger than the amount of pain you inflicted. Alex didn't deserve what happened to him."

"No, he didn't. He's a good and honorable man. And you're right. I owe him an apology—not because I miss him, but because I hurt him. Even if he doesn't accept it, I still want to make it." It's the truth, but it will be so difficult to survive if he rejects me. Probably as difficult as it was for him when my uncle cut Alex's ropes.

"Email me the details of your flight. Gabe will pick you up at the airport."

I promise to send her the details as soon as I have a flight booked and thank her profusely for her advice and assistance. Now I have to figure out how to make an apology as big as he deserves.

I BREAK off from Katherine and Gabe to linger in the shadows. The grand opening crowd is much bigger than the one for the soft opening, but they still clump into groups. The butterflies in my stomach have grown to the size of dragons. My knees shake with each step and turn. If I run into Alex before I'm ready, I could fail miserably. No matter how hard I search, I don't see him.

His lawyer, Zach, is standing next to the man who offered Stone a business card during my walk of shame. Blake, Eliot, and Cade are joined by Graci, the PT from the rehab place, Pierce, and another man who might be the infamous Reed. It's almost too much pretty to take in at once. I slip out of their line of sight. Amy and Tyler have found Katherine and Gabe, and they're having an animated conversation. Gabe and Tyler laugh, so I hope it's not about me.

"I wondered if you'd show up."

I freeze, the air in my lungs turning to lead. Slowly, I will my body to turn and face Stone. He's not surprised at all that I'm here. "Did you send me the invitation?"

"Are you here to make things right?"

"If I can."

"Alex needs a sub for his demo."

"I'm sure he's had multiple volunteers." There are dozens of beautiful women dressed far more daringly than I am in my short black skirt and leather bustier that laces up the front. I spent way too much on a top I might not wear again, but as Katherine reminded me, I only get one shot at this apology.

Stone has somehow led me to the bar. He pulls out a stool. "Hop up."

This is a bad idea. Alex could spot me, and I can't hide. I do it anyway because a worse idea is arguing with Stone.

"This is Cassie."

The cute, curvy bartender gives me a sweet warm smile. She doesn't look old enough to serve, but she must be.

"Would you like something to drink?" Cassie asks.

"No alcohol. She's taking your place for the demo."

"Oh, good." Her relief is palpable. "How about a Coke or water?"

"Water's good."

Cassie bustles around and sets a glass of ice water with a lemon on the lip and a gold-colored flexible straw in front of me.

I pick up the drink. "Even the water is fancy."

"Delivery matters."

I'm not dumb enough to think Stone's talking about the water or even the club.

I nod and agree before sipping my water and searching the crowd for Alex once again.

"He's not here yet. I'll let you know when it's time. You stay here with Cassie."

I open my mouth to agree, but Stone has already turned away to tackle something else that requires his special brand of attention. At least sitting down and getting Stone's assistance has shrunk the dragons in my gut to grasshoppers. I'm still jumpy and nervous but a hell of a lot closer to calm than I was.

Conversation with Cassie happens in a staccato sort of cadence in between her filling drink orders. The curls in her hair bounce along with her. She's like the bubbles in champagne. Going to school for business with an emphasis on human resources. She's doing her classes online so she can save money while she works at the resort. Stone gave her the use of a studio apartment for as long as she's an employee. A twenty-two-year-old has their shit more together than I do. Certainly more than I did at that age. But I'm working on it.

"It's time." Stone's behind me, probably blocking anyone's view of me. "Why don't you freshen up in the ladies' room, and then I'll escort you to the entrance of the stage."

I slip off the stool and quickly cross the distance to the powder room. It's an elegant space with a seating area and full-length mirrors. Behind that first wall are the sinks, and, through another opening, the stalls. I don't have to go—probably slightly dehydrated from being at altitude in this dry climate. I wash my hands. My hair has grown back, but I've kept it short on the sides and back, a little longer on top. I fuss with a couple tendrils. My makeup still looks flawless, which works out since I chose not to bring a bag. Nothing to leave behind but my dignity.

A sharp knock on the door. I open it and find Stone, as I expected.

"Ready?"

"As I'll ever be." I follow behind him, down the elevator, into the dungeon. There's a low EDM track playing, and people have moved to this room while I was hiding out in the bathroom. And now I need to pee. It's nerves. I will the false urge away with a couple of slow deep breaths.

Tyler takes the stage to welcome everyone to the Yacht Club and specifically the dungeon. People are still filing in, not quite as many as there were above but enough to fill the booths and padded chairs that were set up for the demonstrations. When I imagined doing this, there were fewer people. Tyler announces Alex. My first glimpse leaves me breathless. He's shirtless, in black leather pants. Not his jeans. His feet are bare, and his blond hair has been recently cut. Good. God. Damn. The man is fine.

And he hates me.

"...will be joined by his partner for this demo." Tyler glances over to the opposite side of the stage where I've been waiting behind Stone. I step forward. Tyler stutters. "SJ."

Alex's head whips in my direction. I kick off my flats and climb the two stairs barefoot. I've got my skirt undone by the time I make it to the center of the platform. I slide it down my legs and toss it on a padded bench a few feet back. Facing Alex, I slowly unlace my top. I pitch my voice so the crowd can hear me. "Alex is the most talented Shibari master you'll ever have the privilege to see. He's a good and honorable man who works hard. He cares for his friends, and he cares for the women he scenes with. At one time, he cared for me. But I messed that up."

I pull the bustier free and clutch it nervously in my hands.

He hasn't moved. Hasn't said a word.

"I came here tonight to apologize to him and to anyone who saw the spectacle I made of myself at the soft opening." I glance at the crowd. Amy has her hand over her mouth. Katherine is nodding in approval. "I desperately hope that what I did wasn't unforgivable and that Alex will give me a chance to scene with him again." I drop to my knees, press my forearms together and hold them up to him with my head bowed. "To be his little rabbit again. Because I love him."

Silence fills the space. The crowd waits along with me for Alex to respond. The rope drops from his hand to coil on the floor, lifeless. His steps are silent as he walks away, and my heart splits in two again.

"I can't do this," he says to Stone.

I drop my hands and curl into a ball. I fucked this up. I had no right to ask for his forgiveness, especially in public. It seemed like the perfect apology in my head, until it played out. And I can see with complete clarity why he would walk away. Once again, I wish I could take it all back.

Stone comes on stage. Grabs me and my skirt. As soon as I'm clear of the platform, he helps me put my top on. Tyler is back at the microphone, announcing the next demonstration will start shortly and there's a special members-only event coming up. I can't follow the words. All I hear, pounding between my ears, is Alex saying he can't do this.

"Come on." Stone leads me out the back, up the barren stairway painted completely white. We exit from a door behind the kitchen, which is still humming with activity and producing scents that only make my stomach churn harder. He walks over to a golf cart, and I balk.

"I can get a rideshare to the airport."

"I thought you said you love him?" Stone glares at me, peeling away my layers.

"I do. More than he'll ever know."

"If you leave now, that's true. Thought you were more of a fighter than that. You came here tonight dressed for the battle of your life, and you're giving up after one skirmish?"

I hate Stone a little. "Alex said he can't do this."

"He's lying to himself too. Been moping around the Sunflower, staring at the door to the room where you stayed when he walks by. Hasn't done a scene at all since your uncle blew up the soft opening. Dick move, by the way."

"He's known for 'em."

"So he wins. He uses you like a dish rag and tosses you away. Sets Alex up to be railroaded. And you two are letting him make you both miserable. You lied about who you are and what the hell you were doing out here." He points at me, and it's as if he stabbed me in place. "But you had the right reasons, or thought you did."

"I thought he hurt my cousin, who was once my best

friend and is some of the only family I have left. And he has those pictures."

"He uses those, and our lawyers will be up his ass so fast he'll think he's getting a drag race colonoscopy."

I snort laugh. Who knew Stone could be funny? He pats the open space on the bench seat. I walk around the nose of the little cart decked out like a yacht, complete with faux walnut on the dash and a ship's wheel for steering. Kind of cheesy, but I like that they're having some fun with this fancy-pants place.

"Where are we going?" I finally think to ask as we navigate the wide curved sidewalks.

"Alex's place. I'll let you in. You two work it out. A real apology. The knees thing was good. If it was me, I'd say naked and kneeling and dropping a sir as soon as I walk in the door. But Alex doesn't care for that kind of protocol."

No. He's never once asked me to call him anything but Alex. And I don't want to be anything other than his little rabbit. "I'll figure it out."

TWENTY-TWO

ALEX

When I park the truck in my assigned spot outside the condos, the first rays of sunrise are shining over the treetops. The winding roads were almost as tangled as my thoughts about Sarah Jane. The more I drove, the clearer I got. I didn't have to embarrass her in front of everyone. But I can't change it now. I drag my weary ass up the stairs to my second-story home. I'm more brain tired than body tired. Too much thinking. Too much feeling. Nowhere to let it out.

The key turns easily, and my front door slides open soundlessly. There's a light on in the living room that glows into the entry hall. I didn't leave anything on. Out of habit, I take of my boots and stow my hat and my kit bag in the front closet. As soon as I exit the hallway, my heart lurches and my feet stop.

She's here. Naked, kneeling in front of my couch. She's tied a harness around her breasts with the knots perfectly centered over her breastbone. She has laces running the length of her legs, her thighs bulging between the tight symmetrical lines. Her pussy is bare and open to me.

"Whatcha doing, little rabbit?"

"Trying for a better apology. Showing you how much you mean to me. How much I respect you."

I close the distance to her and kneel down, and the tight leather pants Stone demanded I wear squeeze my dick so hard I'm choking. I shift one leg in between hers and take her head in my hands. "I'm sorry I didn't handle things at the club well. Either time."

She shakes her head. "I shouldn't have put you in that situation. Either time. Everything that happened was my fault."

"No, it wasn't." Well, the first time kind of was. But she was lied to by a man who had it out for me for years. I kiss her forehead. "We share some blame. Tonight, you shocked me and I got defensive. But the situation with your uncle... I could have kicked him out. They had no right to be there. I could have made you stay and talk to me. But I'm still figuring out how to have a relationship. An adult one. You know what the first lesson is?"

"What?"

"Honest communication."

She nods. "I'm sorry I lied about who I was."

"I'm sorry I wasn't honest with you about my past and why I had intimacy issues. Trust issues."

She frowns. "I reinforced those."

"You did. But if we're doing this, we're starting with a

clean slate. So is there anything else you need to tell me before I carry you back to my bed and keep you tied up for the next couple days? Because I've missed you so much, little rabbit. Best to tell me now."

"I honestly love you." Her gaze is so clear and open and filled with the love she professes.

"I love you, too, Sarah Jane." I press a kiss to her lips. She rises up on her knees to meet me. It's forgiveness and apology. Promise and devotion. It's love and seduction, and she takes my breath away. I free myself from her possession, holding her cheeks so she can't hide. "What do you want?"

"You. If you'll have me. I want to be your little rabbit."

I shift her so her back is against my chest, and I start freeing her legs. "You've been practicing."

"I missed you. I tried to do the best I can, but it's not the same without you."

I kiss her neck, missing her long hair but loving the access to her skin. "No, it's not."

She arches her back and lifts her arms to put her hands behind my head. Despite the distraction of her perfect breasts, I stay focused on freeing her legs, checking her skin and circulation. Once I'm certain she's fine, I roll her under me. She wraps me in her limbs. I suckle each perfect breast before I say, "Tell me what you need."

"I need to know why you're still wearing pants when you've had access to my naked pussy since you came home. And why leather? I thought you liked your jeans."

I glance down, reminded that wearing these things makes me feel like a sausage in a casing. "I love my jeans. Tyler and Stone ganged up on me. Said I had to look the part for the big event."

"I could help free you."

"God, yes. And you can help me burn them later."

She laughs, and it's the prettiest sound I've ever heard. I manage to get myself upright, and I lift her by the knotted section of her chest harness. She gasps and her eyes half-close.

"I ordered the sexiest bed I could find for this place. Wasn't sure I'd get the chance, but I can use it to make you fly."

"Can't wait."

Unable to resist my caveman urges, I flip her over my shoulder and land a smack to her peach of an ass. Her squeal and kicking legs have me appreciating Tyler's kink a little more. "You know what happens to naughty rabbits who run away?"

"They get tied up and fucked?"

I pop the snap on my pants and lower the zipper to give my cock some room. "Yeah, they get tied up and fucked hard. For days."

She laughs, and I drop her on my new mattress purchased for this bed. The entire metal design is a point of attachment. She's gonna look so good bound there for the rest of the weekend. I drag the leather down my hips. "Hope you don't have any place else to be."

She shakes her head.

"Words."

"No place at all. I'm right where I need to be. Right where I want to be."

I wrestle the pants free of my legs and slap them to the bottom of my closet while I grab two new ropes hanging there. When I turn around, Sarah Jane is spread eagle, that wet, sexy pussy calling to me.

"Safe words."

"Yellow and red."

I make use of her perfectly tied harness and secure each leg so it's bent and open, leaving her fully exposed. "I'm gonna eat this pussy until you beg me to stop. And then I'm going to fuck you until the sun rises."

"Yes, Alex."

I shift her around on the bed, making room for me to keep my promise. A long lap at her sweet entrance, and I'm gone like I've taken the best drug. She's right where I want her to be, and so am I. With my face buried in her pussy, she squeals and begs. I screw two fingers deep in her channel and suck her clit like she's between me and the last sip of my milkshake. She explodes and tries to roll away. I secure her with my arm across her belly and take her there again. Two more, and she's soft and pliable. "Ready to fly, little rabbit?"

"I thought I already did."

"Not yet, but you will."

I take my time preparing the suspension, making sure she'll hang at the perfect height from the side frame. I'll be able to stand and move her exactly as I want. She watches me intently. The anticipation builds between us.

Her tongue flicks across her lips as I connect her harness to my lead. "Trust me?"

"Always. With everything." She says the words I needed to hear more than I'm sorry. After all the shit that passed between us, I realize, I trust her too. To be honest like she was on that stage, to make things right like she did with the lawyer and her cousin, to be the little rabbit I've dreamed of having in my life.

"Deep breath."

She sucks in air, and as she releases, I lift her, suspend her from the bed to the perfect height to fuck her. She floats there, in my ropes, open. Wet. Willing. Wrangled. I slowly walk around the bed, centered in the huge bedroom. She's beautiful from every angle, and she's mine. I stop long enough to roll on a condom, and then I'm back where I belong with my dick teasing her entrance.

"Please, Alex. Fuck me."

I swing her forward down my length. Deeply seated and unable or unwilling to move because that would mean leaving the only place that feels more like home than home. I fall into her gaze. She's got me as tightly bound as I have her.

Her pussy clamps down, and she says, "Yes."

Not sure what my soul asked her, but I have a suspicion. Someday soon, I'll ask her for real. I swing her back a tiny bit and then right back into place. For now I ask, "Come home with me for Christmas?"

"You sure?"

I swing her back down my length and forward,

somehow even deeper. I barely keep my eyes from rolling back in my head, she feels so good. "Never been more sure in my life."

"Then yes."

I shift her by the shoulders and kiss her until we're both breathless. She's boneless in my ropes as I take her hard, make her scream, and explode into her. By the time I release her from her ropes and mine, I'm hard again.

I try to keep my word to fuck her into the next sunrise, but I give out after the second round of sweet vanilla lovemaking.

I make good on my promise to fuck her for days.

And to love her for all the days.

EPILOGUE

BLAKE

"Well, that was awkward." I've never seen Alex deliberately be rude but leaving SJ on the stage like that was brutal. Tyler's doing a great job of managing the crowd, but Alex's was the demo I wanted to see.

"What now?" Reed glances around, still acting like a cat with tape on his feet—not sure where to settle.

Eliot and Cade flank Graci. I can't believe she came. And in that dress. The woman is hotter than a sun flare in scrubs. In the tiny black dress with a zipper that runs top to bottom down the front of her body, she is total temptation. The guys haven't taken their eyes off her. Looks like they might invite her to a private room. Good for them. Except once again, I'll be left on the sidelines.

"Graci, would you like a drink?" Cade asks, clasping her hand to get her complete focus. He's the most emotional of all of us. Well, Eliot, Cade, Reed, and me. The original Four Winds Security. I'm still not sure how

Pierce fits in. Cool dude. Helpful, but there is no fifth wind. Unless everyone has figured out I'm never going to be the same. Can't exactly soar in a wheelchair. Maybe Pierce is here to replace me.

"Club soda, with lime?" Graci's soft tone barely carries over the background music.

"Of course," Cade replies.

"I'll go with you," Pierce says, following Cade to the bar.

I'd love to roll away, but the guys will make a big deal of trailing me, and Graci will fuss. I slump down and scowl. Back in the day, we'd be figuring out how to get Graci in bed with us. All of us. The four of us. Instead of dancing around, awkward as ass, not knowing how to move as a team. And that's on me. I'm the fucking problem. The variable in the equation that no longer works. I'm the bug in the code. "You guys should fuck her."

"What? Who?" Eliot asks as if it wasn't on his mind.

"You, Cade, Reed, and Pierce should invite Graci back to a private room. That is why you invited her here, isn't it? I get that I'm in a wheelchair. I've lost the use of my legs, but I haven't fucking lost my mind."

"When did you get so damn surly?" Reed asks. "And why Graci? And Pierce?" He crosses his arms. "Found someone to fill my shoes, El?"

Eliot snaps his focus from me to Reed. "What is that supposed to mean?"

"I've been stuck in St. Louis. Come out here, and Pierce is hanging around, playing errand boy. But then he's here on opening night. Does he have a bedroom in the condo? Do I?"

"You can bunk with me at the rehab. My mouth still works." I've missed Reed and sex.

"Nobody is bunking at rehab. And yes, I'd like Pierce to stay with us. But only if we all agree."

Reed turns his back on Eliot. "You used me."

"I did not." Eliot goes to him, a hand on Reed's shoulder. "I relied on you to take care of us while Blake recovers. And you did. You always do. Why in hell would you think you could be replaced? Same goes for you." Eliot glares back at me. "Why in the world would you think we want to replace either of you?"

It's nice lip service, but I won't be walking again. My contribution to the business is still possible on some level, but being anyone's lover... That ship has sailed. Proven by the fact none of them has made any kind of move on me in a year. I can't even masturbate since my dick doesn't get hard.

Cade, Pierce, and Graci return. Her lips on the straw, sipping her drink, is enough to push me into some filthy thoughts. Me eating her out while she sucks off one of the guys and gets fucked by two more. Still have one too many players in the scenario. Reed's right, we don't fit together the same way. But then my mind puts Pierce on his knees, sucking me. The tingle that trails down my back is a shadow of what I once felt, but fuck, it feels good to have that much.

"I want to show you something." Eliot directs his words to the entire group, but his gaze lands on me.

Your dick? "Sure."

"I can hang out here," Graci says.

"No, you're coming too." Eliot turns for the elevator. Guess there's no argument. But I still wait to see what she's going to do.

"Guess we're going," she says to me.

I shrug. What do I care?

She bends down and asks, "Can I drive?"

She can do whatever the fuck she wants to me as long as she stays so close I can smell the cinnamon tease of her skin and feel her breath on my neck. "Sure."

"Hold this?" She hands me her glass, and I take it. I'd like to hold her anything. Her everything. Use my mouth over her entire body until she's screaming and quaking under me, over me, beside me. I don't care about the position. That's her job to get me where she wants me. If she'd let me, it would be my job to make her come morning, noon, and night.

We ride the elevator up and trail the guys out of the restaurant. It's a beautiful, crisp mountain night. The air is alive with the scent of trees and earth, nothing like the institutional air I've been breathing for the past year. It cools some of my anger. Is it even anger? More like righteous indignation at everything that was stolen from me last year. Some days, I wonder why I bothered to live. Less since I met Graci, but I'm still angry. Maybe more so since I met her and can't have her. Not only because of the dick sitch, but because she's my physical therapist. There are lines we can't cross.

"Where're we going, Eliot?" I ask.

"You'll see, Grumpy."

I scowl, but it's wasted on his back. Finally, we get to the finished four-story building that holds the condos. The upper floor sold out nearly instantly, according to Tyler. He and Amy are managing the housing part of the resort—sales and rentals. The demand is huge. I'll get my investment back easily, with a large return. Graci guides me up the ramp to the sliding doors that open automatically. The hallways are tiled in what looks like hardwood panels. The place is elegant. Amy has great taste.

"Here we are." Eliot stops at a door on the ground floor. "You want to do the honors?"

Graci takes her drink. I roll myself forward and place my palm on the sensor, part of the security system I selected. The panel turns green, and the door swings open. The guys step back and let me roll through first into a huge open-concept living space. As I enter, the lights turn on, and I see a huge U-shaped sofa fills the living area with a wall-mounted TV bigger than the windows. There's even a gas fireplace. In my past life, this would be the place we would all get together and let what happens between us happen. Well, here or the bedroom. But no one has touched me like that since the accident.

"Dim," Eliot says behind me, and the light brightness decreases. "Everything is either voice activated or at an accessible height."

His words hit me like a gut punch. They don't believe I'll ever be out of this chair. Air backs up in my lungs. The urge to destroy something or someone rises to a point I can hardly resist. I fucking hate my life.

Graci's fingertips graze my shoulder, and I exhale. "Show me your room?"

If only that was the invitation my mind twists it to be. "Where's my room?"

Eliot points at another door. "Through there."

The sensor works exactly like the front door, and the door swings open. "Why the internal security?"

"Fire safety. Still two units in the plans."

Cade, Pierce, and Reed have disappeared to the back hall, so it's Graci and I who enter the second part of the condo. The kitchen is smaller, lower. Chair height. I should be thrilled with the mods they put in for me. Instead, I'm sick. The living room is set up like a workout room.

Like a physical therapy space.

"Nice," Graci says, setting her glass on the kitchen counter.

"Another place for you to torture me."

"Someone. I'll be four hours away."

Is it wishful thinking, or does her voice sound kind of wistful?

"Let's find my bedroom."

There are two, both with bathrooms attached. It's clear mine is the bigger one, based on the roll-in shower. "They thought of everything."

Graci steps into the shower under a rain head I hadn't noticed at first. She mimes washing her hair, her body moving to an internal sinuous beat. Naked. My brain supplies an image of her, wet, without clothes. I roll forward. We both fit in the space. She smiles, and my dick twitches.

Holy fuck.

It was tiny. No stiffy, but it twitched.

"So Graci, you staying the night with us?" Eliot's deep, sexy baritone echoes in the tiled space.

I didn't see him come in, and he's trailed by the rest of the guys. Graci is blocked inside the shower because I'm in the entrance. I don't move. She's mine.

No. She's not.

And I haven't had a problem with sharing before.

Who am I?

I roll out of the shower, pushing Eliot and the guys back. She steps out and takes my hand. Hers trembles slightly in my grip. There's nothing forcing her to stay. She could have a hotel booked or a room at the resort for all I know. She hasn't said a word.

I glance up. Her deep brown eyes meet mine. "What do you want to do, Graci?"

She lifts her chin, checks out the guys, and returns to me. Sadder now. "I can't. I have to go."

I release her hand. The guys part, giving her an aisle of escape. She darts through them like she's running a gauntlet. A hollowness settles in my chest.

Eliot follows her out, but the rest of the guys are staring at me with varying shades of pity.

"Get the fuck out of my room. I need some sleep." I don't recognize my own voice, but I'm fine when they depart. I don't need them up my ass. Literally or figuratively. And I don't need Graci offering me attention out of pity.

ACKNOWLEDGMENTS

First, last, and always, thank you to my husband for supporting my writing in every way. I love you!

Thank you to the Red Reines—Carol Potenza, Ryley Banks, and Erin Krueger—for everything you do.

Thank you to Brandi Doane McCann for another amazing cover and the fabulous series logo.

Thank you to Dayna Hart and Jenny Rardon for the fantastic editing. Readers, please know that any errors you find while reading this book are mine, not theirs. I'm incorrigible.

Thank you to my amazing beta readers who made this book infinitely better.

Thank you to Passionate Ink for providing a safe and educational forum for erotic authors.

Grateful love to the authors mentioned or eluded to in this book, including: Cecilia Tan, Raisa Greywood, Marie Tuhart, Finley Fenn, and Maggie Sims for writing books my characters (and I) love to read.

And, most importantly, thank you to my readers who make it worth all the struggles to write!

ABOUT THE AUTHOR

Award-winning, best-selling author, Jordyn Kross, is an unapologetically naughty novelist who spent years honing her writing skills with tech manuals and marginal poetry before finding her passion for writing sexy, boundary-stretching happily-ever-afters.

When she's not writing, she's attempting to garden in the desert Southwest, hiking with her insane pound posse, and admiring that handsome man wandering around her house who continues to stay.

Jordyn enjoys saucy double entendres, pretending to be an extrovert, and is well-known for having no filter. And when she's not in social media jail, she can be found on Facebook, Instagram, and BookBub, or hiding in a dark cave peering out at the X file formerly knows as Twitter.